Heart of Curiosities

Curiosity Bay Series #1

Karice Bolton

Edited by V. Clifton

Cover Design: Didi
Adobe Stock: © LukaszDesign

Interior: B&B Formatting
Adobe Stock: © beaubelle

DEDICATION

To My Fantastic Readers. Thank you for making these stories come to life!

To my Family. You are my everything!

CHAPTER ONE

Amelia

The sunlight flirted with the tapestry of clouds rolling over Curiosity Bay while I silently begged for a few more hours of brilliant blue skies to hover overhead. The summer storm rolling in would stop our progress, and we had plenty to do.

I puffed out air between my lips and spun around to see my three sisters staring at a box of curiosities wedged on top of a table underneath our green and white striped store awning. Our antique shop had been in our family for decades, but it sometimes felt like I was the only one who wanted to be there. Well, except for Dottie.

Our town's honorary mascot loved basking in the spotlight with her pugalicious self. She was also the only female in our family, apart from my mom, who had fantastic luck with the opposite sex. Seated under the table by my sisters, Dottie stretched her tan paws and wiggled her curled tail, followed by her infamous snort. She'd just returned from the dog park and was feeling extra proud of herself.

My oldest sister, Mae, glanced up at me while tucking a stray piece of dark hair behind her ear. Even though my mom did a fabulous job of popping us out every two years, we'd managed to look like quintuplets, four sisters with dark hair and green eyes and a brother with the same. If you lined us up in front of the antique store, it would be hard for anyone to tell us apart, except that our brother now had a beard.

But we couldn't be more different.

"How many more boxes of junk do we have to go through before the rain hits us?" Mae asked while my sister Emily prodded her side with an elbow.

"Don't get Amelia all fired up. This isn't junk," Emily whispered. "These are *treasures*."

Audrey snickered, and I scowled at the three troublemakers. I'd say four troublemakers, but Dottie already fell asleep on us. I might be the youngest, but I felt more mature than all of them combined.

Albeit, that wasn't saying much.

"This is only the beginning. The estate sale was ginormous," I said with a smile.

"Ginormous, huh?" Audrey teased.

"Two portable storage units are being delivered this week, so yeah. Ginormous." I winked, knowing that would shut them up with plenty of work on the horizon.

A catcall whistled down the street, and we all looked over to see Bryce with his Doberman walking toward us.

"Is that really appropriate?" I teased.

His eyes sparkled, and he glanced at Dottie. "It was on behalf of Herman. You know he's got a thing for that pug."

My sisters chuckled as Bryce and his dog walked down the street toward the post office. It was a daily ritual. Bryce was a good guy, single... and more than ready to mingle with one of my sisters, but we knew too much about him. He was the kid who ate everything you weren't supposed to eat in kindergarten, which wasn't what bothered us. Hey, whatever floats your boat at that age, but once he started sticking the mysterious things in our lunchboxes, all bets were off. We never forgave him.

I walked over to my sisters and peered into the box in question. It looked like somebody had dumped an old junk drawer into a cardboard box and shaken it up a bit, evidenced by a few red buttons, some coins, and a chipped ceramic spoon rest.

My eyes caught a light-green reflection at the bottom of the box, and my heart puttered a little quicker. I dug away the heavy objects to carefully pull out a center-handle sandwich plate in the Cameo pattern that was all the rage right now.

"You've got to be kidding me," Mae said with a wry smile. "How did you spot that?"

"Oh, you mean this little four-thousand-dollar gem?" I teased, feeling the cold, smooth glass between my fingertips.

"No way is that four grand," Audrey said, shaking her head.

"That's what the last one went for at auction. Depression glass is super popular right now, and this is a rare piece."

Mae nodded a quick confirmation. "At *least* that much money in your hands. You have a real eye for this, Amelia."

"Thanks. It's what I do." I playfully rolled my eyes.

It's all I've got was more what it felt like. I'd struck out in the love department more times than I cared to admit. I'd lost my best friend of twenty years when she ran away with my boyfriend three years ago. The apartment building I'd lived in for ten years caught fire four months ago and had been demolished as of last week, and my trusty ride of eleven years finally gave its last wheeze three days ago.

So, yeah. Finding the diamonds in the rough was what I did best. It started as a hobby as a kid at my parents' antique store, which turned into an after-school job during my teen years before going to college and getting my degree in history. Then, our family store, Baubles and Curiosities, beckoned me back, and here I was with the mindset that I was planted for the duration.

I noticed Audrey checking her phone.

"Have a hot date tonight?" I joked.

"As a matter of fact, I do." She blushed, and her green eyes brightened a smidge. "I need to catch the ferry in thirty minutes."

"What are you waiting for? Amelia, Emily, and I can finish up." Mae shooed her away from the box. "It's not every day we have a reason to get off the island on a Friday night."

I nodded in agreement, still clutching the glass. If I were to be completely honest with myself, which I didn't enjoy doing too much because living in a bubble of fantasy was a bit more fun and a lot less complicated, I might envy my sisters' abilities to put themselves out there.

Just a little.

But I was seldom honest with myself, so I was pretty sure I wasn't actually jealous of much, especially when it came to getting a heart broken because that was inevitable once you opened the door.

"Don't do anything I wouldn't do," I called after my sister as I bounded into the antique store where my mom was dusting behind the counter to the left.

Did I mention we looked exactly like my mom? My dad had blond hair and hazel eyes, but if he stood in the light just right, there was a tinge of green, which he claimed tied us all together.

I heard a snort from behind and saw Dottie on the move to her next resting station. Life was good for that pug in her green mini-shawl my mom had whipped up for her to keep the chill away.

"Is that what I think it is?" My mom straightened and shoved her emerald-green shawl over her right shoulder, knocking a dangling, sterling silver earring in the process. Yes, her shawl matched Dottie's. Always did. Every. Single. Day. Another thing was that we all had an affinity for the costume jewelry that came in here. It might possibly be a downfall of ours someday.

My mom also loved living in the past, which explained why she'd named her children after memorable

6

figures in American culture. Amelia Earhart for me. Emily Dickinson for my next oldest sister. Audrey Hepburn for the second to oldest sister, and finally, Mae West, who started the naming tradition. My brother, who was technically the second oldest sibling, was named after Marlon Brando, but everybody wound up calling him Brad, and I really had no idea why. Maybe my parents figured out that being named after a fish when you live on an island is too much for other kids to handle. Granted, the fish is spelled with an *i* and not an *o*, but kids wouldn't care.

I placed the green glass on the counter, and she smiled. "You have the magic touch. The vision."

Chuckling, I shook my head. My mom always loved to believe her children held superpowers.

"If the junk box indicates what's to come from this bulk estate sale, we might have really scored." I grinned, glancing at my sisters coming inside.

"Did I just hear Amelia call this a junk box?" Mae chuckled, shaking the contents. "Is the world ending?"

"So, what do you girls have planned for your Friday night?" my mom asked, eyeing each of us individually.

"Audrey has a date in Seattle. She's already headed to the ferry." Emily shrugged. "As for me, I'm headed to Milo's."

Even though it sounded like she had a date with a man, Milo's was actually one of the local pubs we had here on the island. It wasn't unusual for Emily to go kick it up on the weekend as much as one could on Marigold Island.

"I'm working on the final details for the coffee shop," Mae explained. "It's only three months out, and they'll be breaking through this wall next month to add the access between the two places."

"It's going to be so cool." I nodded, glancing at one of the unopened boxes from the estate sale sitting behind a curio cabinet. "My entire paycheck will probably go toward lattes and mochas."

My mom's gaze caught mine. "What about you?"

"I plan on opening up a few more boxes, grabbing a take-and-bake pizza, and curling up with a good book."

She rolled her eyes. "You're so my daughter."

"I take offense." Mae chuckled, knowing she was more like our dad than any of us.

"What about you guys?" I waggled my brows at my mom. "You and Dad going on a hot date tonight?"

"We're headed over to the Millers' for bridge. Do with that information what you will, but I'm guessing I'll get to bed early and wind up with a wine headache for tomorrow morning."

"At least I'm the one opening the store in the early a.m." I chuckled, loving how my parents still made time for one another. They'd been married for thirty-eight years and acted like it had been ten. The funny thing was that I'd thought I had that too. You know, before my BFF took off with my fiancé. Oh, did I forget to mention we'd been engaged?

But I was so over it.

Really.

Possibly.

Maybe, someday.

Emily turned off the *Open* sign and propped the door just as the thunder rumbled through the air. The electricity combed over my skin, and I knew our sorting time had abruptly ended.

We scurried outside and brought the remaining boxes inside before locking the front door. And within minutes, a flurry of activity whirled around me, with coats and purses grabbed, most lights shut off, and a pug tucked under my mom's arm.

My mom double-tapped a statue of Artemis, which had belonged to my grandma, and then kissed her fingers afterward. It was tradition. She was certain my grandma still graced the figurine's presence, or maybe it was the other way around. Our family had lots of little quirks like that. It wasn't that we were necessarily superstitious or mystic, but there were plenty of times when someone in the family thought they had a special…*power*, and let's just say none of us ever wanted to rain on someone's parade.

For instance, each of my siblings and I have a vintage item my mom handpicked upon birth that she felt told her something about our potential life partners. I received a broach. Emily got a necklace. Mae received a pair of earrings. Audrey got a hairpin. Brad had a watch. To this day, my mom swore up and down that each of those items would give us some hint about whom we should wind up with. Being that we were all very clearly single, it wasn't something we brought up often.

The thought made me chuckle as my family gave one last group wave and wandered out the back.

This was always one of my favorite times. I liked to linger and very rarely wanted to hurry anywhere. The smell of well-loved books drifted through the air, and the mannequins draped in vintage lace anchored the aisles along with Art-Deco and Mid-Century Modern clocks ticking a tale that I could finally let my mind imagine. This was my favorite part about working in an antique store. I'd touch a piece and imagine who held it last, what their life meant to their loved ones, the legacy they left behind, and the mystery that remained. It was downright exhilarating.

That was why I had to open the box that I'd been eyeing all day. I'd placed it behind a curio cabinet to ensure I'd get first dibs. There was something about the worn cardboard that just called to me. I'd had this feeling before where my fingers and toes tingled with anticipation, and the sensation always led to good things.

I grabbed a box cutter from behind the counter and tore into the cardboard.

"Ouch," I hissed to myself as the blade ran across my skin. I glanced at the tiny slash, sucked on it for a second, and put my shirt over it to stop the bleeding.

I ripped the tape to shreds without the razor blade, and the cardboard flaps sprang open.

A pop of dazzling turquoise caught my eye as I focused on the earthenware vase packed carefully between Styrofoam. The tingling sensation zipped through me as I recognized the color Theodore Deck's pieces were known for. He'd developed a beautiful glazing technique in the late Nineteenth Century with vivid colors like this exact turquoise lying in front of me.

But there was no way we could luck out with the sandwich plate *and* a vase by Deck.

No way.

Not our little antique store in the middle of nowhere off the coast of Washington State.

My trembling hands raised the turquoise vase, which I turned over to see a signature.

TH Deck.

With wide eyes, I placed it back down and noticed several folded bundles of paper had fallen from the vase. Each one had been tied with a piece of twine.

I picked up the vase again and brought it to my right eye when it sounded like something else rattled inside. I spotted a tiny book, maybe a diary or address book, shoved inside. I shook the vase, hoping it would fall out. My hand was definitely too large to shove inside the narrow opening. But I had these letters and could start there.

A little bit of guilt pricked its way through me as I eyed the stack of neatly tied bunches. Technically, everything we bought was ours, so I did have a right to open one of the bundles and read whatever was written.

I twisted my lips into a contemplative pout as my fingers touched the rough string. A tingle spread through me, and without another thought, I untied the top packet. The paper felt old but not ancient. The vase had done a good job of protecting the stationery over the years. As I unfolded the top paper, that little irritating speck of guilt surfaced again, especially when I started to read the letter.

My Dear Little JJ,

My star baseball player, talented artist, and best speller in the state, your dreams will always be my dreams. I love you more than you could ever imagine, and I can't wait to watch you grow up to be an incredible and absolutely lovely man. But right now, you're my little JJ, and I'm cherishing all the snuggles we have together.

With all my love,
Mommy

I didn't know JJ or his mother, but my throat clenched as love surged through these words, and I knew I needed to return these letters to their rightful owner. Folding the letter back to how I'd found it, I kicked myself when I realized a dot of my blood had smudged the paper.

Nonetheless, I dashed to the counter and looked over the information from the estate sale. There weren't any names listed with J as a contact, only some management firm.

My foot tapped with impatience as I logged onto the computer and attempted to look up the management group.

Still, no man with a J on any part of the website or contacts. If I couldn't find him, my sister could. I sent her a quick text to ensure she was still at Milo's, and she sent a thumbs-up emoji back.

I let out a little growl, quickly gathered the letters, and put them back in the vase before moving the box into the back room so everything didn't accidentally get sold in the morning.

After closing up the rest of the antique store, flipping off the remaining lights, and setting the alarm, I made my way to the car I'd borrowed from my parents until I made my way to Seattle to find a new one.

Another round of thunder clapped not far from the shoreline as I turned onto the main road toward Milo's. Just as I entered the parking lot, the rain started dumping, and a shiver found its way through my spine even though it wasn't a degree below seventy. I scurried into the pub overlooking crashing waves against the dock with boats bobbing to prove the weathermen wrong once more. This wasn't a little storm.

"Ah, if it isn't the elusive Evans sister," the bartender called the moment I entered the pub.

I frowned as the entire place turned and raised whatever they were drinking in my direction. My cheeks flamed red, and I spotted my sister in a far booth with a book.

Not quite what I pictured Emily to be doing whenever she announced her Friday night plans at Milo's.

I hid a little snicker and made my way over to Emily, who was one of the few who didn't hear the bartender's greeting.

"A little absorbed in the story?" I teased as Emily's gaze flashed to mine.

"What are you doing here?"

"I told you I was coming."

"No, you asked if I was still here."

I shrugged and slid into the booth with my little bundle as she closed her book. "And all this time, I thought you were dancing on the bar and whooping it up with the bartender with drinks spilling out of your mugs."

"You watch too much reality television." Emily chuckled and slid her book away as the server brought over a basket of garlic cheese fries sprinkled with Parmesan.

"Want some?" she asked, pushing the basket toward me.

Every single thing I thought I knew about my sister got blown to smithereens, and I think she realized it. Emily always had a way of making us think she was a party animal, living it up on her Friday nights while the rest of us stayed home.

I pursed my lips together before heaving a sigh. "So, I need your help."

Her brows pulled up. "With what… and why are you bleeding? You've only been alone for less than an hour."

I chuckled. "It was a box cutter this time."

Emily rolled her eyes with a grin. "Of course it was. I feel like there should be a list of tools you're not allowed to use unless you have someone with you."

"Hardee-har-har."

"I'm totally not kidding."

I set the folded bundle of letters with the twine on top of the table and let out a deep breath. "Well, I found a vase with letters inside and something else I can't actually fish out of the ceramic without damaging it.

"Okay…What does that have to do with me?"

"Well, I read the first letter, and I know whomever they're meant for needs to read them and keep them. The problem is that I only know that I'm looking for a man with a name that starts with J, and the company who managed the estate sale has no information with that name."

"Your plan is to hunt down some random guy to hand him a pack of letters stuck in a vase?"

I nodded and stole a fry. "Yup, and I need your help. You're a master sleuth when it comes to tracking people down."

She pressed her lips together and frowned. "Why do you say that?"

I chuckled. "Really? Do I need to explain your ability to sniff out any potential online issues with guys we go out with? It's probably why I'm still single. Men are duds."

It was the truth. Somehow, Emily had this unnatural and uncanny ability to find out anything and everything about someone. Things we didn't even want to know. All it took was a name, and she'd handle the rest. I think Mae still hadn't recovered from the man she almost went on a blind date with who had an entire family on the East Coast.

"The vase is actually really rare. Same estate sale as the sandwich plate, so I'm guessing whomever the items came from was well-to-do." I sighed and gently untied the bundle again. "But these letters have got to get to that little boy."

"Who might not be so little. Thank goodness names with J aren't common," she said wryly.

"I know it's crazy, but I think these letters really need to get to him."

Emily took the letter I'd opened and read it, touching her chest in the meantime. "Oh, my gosh. That is beautiful."

I nodded. "And there are many more. I just didn't feel right reading them."

She plucked an extra cheesy fry off the top as Rick, another bartender, came over.

"How's the meal?" he asked, eyeing Emily.

"Delicious as always." She grinned, turning her attention to him. He was well over six feet tall and not only made the drinks here, but he also actually owned the pub and the building he ran it from.

"Good. Always like to hear it." He glanced at me and then back at my sister. "Are you free tomorrow afternoon?"

Rick towered over us with his dark hair and gleaming blue eyes as he waited for my sister to respond. Was that why Emily always came to Milo's? She had a thing for Rick?

"I'm actually working tomorrow."

I shook my head, knowing it was only Audrey and me on duty, until I felt a swift ankle kick and kept my mouth shut.

One thing to know about me was that I had a tendency to try to be overly helpful, and apparently, this was one of those times.

Rick's expression fell, and he nodded. "Maybe next time."

Emily smiled and nodded as he trundled away. She grabbed her phone and started typing.

"What was that all about?" I whispered.

"He keeps asking me out."

"Is that because you keep showing up on Friday nights to read a book?"

She snickered and stared at her cell phone.

"Are you going to help or not?" I asked, feeling a desperate itch to find JJ.

"What do you think I'm doing?" She grabbed another fry.

Within minutes, a droll grin spread across Emily's face, and her eyes widened. "Whoa. If this is the J we are looking for, I'll happily hand-deliver any letters needed."

I chuckled and shook my head. "Are you serious? You found an option that quickly?"

"I can't be sure it's him, but there was an obituary from six months ago that listed a J. Edwards as the only son, and the family was very prominent. They're an old timber family who also owned some orchards and sold some secret family recipe to one of the big beverage companies before buying it back and producing it themselves."

"How could you find this in less than five minutes?" My pulse quickened with excitement. Could this really be him?

"It's not that hard." Emily shrugged. "I could be wrong, but I doubt it."

"Let me see," I nearly squealed.

She clutched her phone and eyed me. "Are you sure you can handle this?"

"What are you talking about? I'm just trying to give a man some letters from his mom."

"Fair warning. He's our age, attractive, and…"

"And what?"

She flipped the phone around, and my mouth hung open in surprise.

CHAPTER TWO

James

"How many times is this woman going to call?" I glanced at another message my assistant stuck on my desk.

"Who is she?" My cousin Lucas stood near the window in my office overlooking the small bay on Woodley Island. Lucas turned to face me with an eager-looking glint in his eyes.

I cocked my head and stared at him in disbelief. All it took was the word *woman* to surface on his radar, and he was ready to pounce.

"Some lady who owns an antique store."

"Ooph. That's brutal." My cousin knew what I was thinking. Snakes and pariahs always circled to get something from our family. "Didn't you get everything all taken care of from your mom's estate?"

I nodded, crumpling the paper and tossing it into the garbage.

My grandparents had essentially raised me, but they'd ensured that their daughter, my mother, was always taken care of too. But when she got ill, my grandparents were no longer here, and I had to come face to face with the fact that I needed to care for someone who'd never cared for me, but she passed away before I ever had the chance.

But I'd put that all behind me.

Sliding a chair out from my desk, I took a seat and waited for Lucas to do the same.

"It's Monday evening. The sun is shining after a stormy weekend on your sailboat, and I say it's time to make up for lost time."

I laughed and shook my head. "I'm not going out with you tonight."

"Why's that? Already have plans?" he asked. "This whole recluse vibe really gets old. I want my old James back."

"I'm not a recluse, I'm a dad. My son will be here any second. The nanny is dropping him off soon."

"And I bet Henry would love to hear some live music and scarf down some fries."

"So, now you want to use my three-year-old as a

wingman?"

"It's a sure thing to help my night go smoothly."

I shook my head and groaned. "You need to give it up. Henry wants nothing more than to go home, put his feet up on the couch, and have some macaroni and cheese."

"Are you talking about Henry or yourself?"

I smiled. "We're the same man."

At times, it truly felt like that. Henry was my number one reason for existing. He made my world go around, and I couldn't imagine not spending every waking second with him.

"I promise I'll leave you alone the rest of the week if you and Henry come out to dinner tonight." He sighed. "All you do is work or hide out at home or on your sailboat."

He wasn't giving up.

"Again, I'm not hiding out. I'm having a blast with my little guy."

All because he wanted me to be his wingman. That truly was what all this was about. He didn't care whether I found a woman or not. He needed me to be by his side while he scoped for his next girlfriend.

"I don't think that's entirely true. I just think sometimes, he's a convenient excuse to stay in."

I laughed. "Which I'll happily do until he's tired of me."

"You're almost thirty-eight. Before you know it, you're going to throw your back out putting on a sock, and the rest will be downhill from there." Lucas grinned salaciously, but I had to love him. He was the only male cousin I had, and he also happened to be my best friend. "When was the last time you've even been to our grandparents' house on Marigold Island?"

I let out a deep sigh and closed my laptop, deciding to answer one question so I could dodge the other. "Fine. We'll go with you tonight, but you have to promise to leave me alone the rest of the week."

Lucas' expression fell. "I can't promise that after all."

My office phone rang, and I absentmindedly picked it up on speakerphone.

"James speaking."

A woman sucked in a deep breath, and I glanced at Lucas, who eyed me.

"Is…is this Mr. James Edwards?"

Crap. My assistant already went home, and security at the front desk probably just patched this person through, thinking it would go to voicemail.

"Speaking."

My cousin flinched from the gruffness in my voice, and I smiled.

24

"Hi. I'm from Baubles and Curiosities over on…"

Uneasiness lurked as I drew a breath. The number of times my family had been taken advantage of outmoded anything this woman had to say. It was just history repeating itself—another day, another time.

"We've already taken care of everything," I told the woman briskly.

"But I'm certain—"

"What we didn't sell, I donated. Have a nice evening." I hung up the phone and rolled my eyes as Lucas stared at me.

"She sounded hot."

I scowled at my cousin. "Are you serious?"

"Deadly. I mean, this girl sounded like exotic supermodel hot."

I scratched the scruff on my chin and chuckled. "What planet did you come from, and can we send you back?"

Lucas stood. "Come on. You can't tell me she didn't sound insanely gorgeous to you?"

"You mean with the three words she spoke trying to buy low from our family and sell high?"

Lucas laughed and raised his shoulders slightly. "Everyone's gotta make a living."

"Would you like me to track her down on Caller ID

and get her number for you?" I joked. "Or I could tape the Post-It notes back together from the trash for you."

"I wouldn't turn it down." He walked behind my desk, kicked my chair around to face the window, and shook me from behind. "I have a confession."

"What's that?" I stood, knowing the sooner I went out with Lucas, the sooner I could get home.

"I've been in a drought."

"A drought?"

He nodded and sighed as if the world might be ending. "It's been three weeks."

"Three weeks since what?"

We walked out of my office.

"I haven't held a girl in three weeks."

I spun around and stopped to stare at my cousin. "Three weeks is not a drought. Three months, probably not…Three years, sure."

He clapped my shoulder and grinned. "You need to get back in the game, man."

"I've never been in the game." It wasn't exactly a secret that I avoided relationships at all costs, and it wasn't merely romantic relationships that I tended to run away from either. I wasn't great at the whole people thing.

But I assumed that when you grew up like I did, it was

common to have a few trust issues. Absent parents and boarding schools weren't exactly what screamed warmth and stability, and then what happened with Henry's mother just made me give up entirely on the prospect.

I shook my head as we started toward the lobby and Mary appeared with my son.

Just the sight of Henry made me feel like I was floating on cloud nine. There was something about his round cheeks and flippy hair that just made any sour day turn sweet.

I knelt down and opened my arms. "How's my boy? Was preschool everything you hoped and more?"

Henry chuckled, burying his head into my chest as I hugged him. His giggles filled the air. I was such a lucky father. He took a step back and looked at Lucas, whom he calls Uncle Luke.

"Hi, Uncle Luke." Henry beamed. "I drew you."

Mary laughed and nodded. "That is true. His preschool teacher handed me this masterpiece when we were leaving."

My cousin smiled and wandered over to take a look.

I held in my laugh as I looked at the man with no neck, four arms, three legs, and no eyes. But Uncle Luke did have two mouths.

"Nice, li'l buddy. You're a regular Picasso."

"Who's Scappo?" Henry's brows furrowed as he stared at his uncle.

Lucas smiled. "Just a famous artist. Guess what I convinced your dad to do?"

Henry turned to look at me. "What?"

"I'm taking you for fries and a live band. What do you say?"

Henry shrugged and looked at me. "MacCheese?"

"We can get some later," I promised, which eased Henry's mind. "Thanks for taking him to preschool this morning, Mary. The meeting this morning was way earlier than it should have been."

"He's a pleasure." She bent down to Henry and patted his head. "I'll see you tomorrow after school."

"Bye-bye." Henry twisted his fingers to wave as Mary left.

"So, where are we headed?" I glanced at my cousin, who was grinning from ear to ear. "And what's the plan?"

"You can play the strong and silent type," he told me as I walked to my car. "And I'll be the guy everybody loves, who's doting on his adorable nephew."

"Not quite what I meant, but fine."

"We're headed to Griffin's." He got into his car, and I nodded.

"Uncle Luke is silly." Henry giggled as I put him into his car seat in the back.

"Yes, he is." I tightened the strap and shut the door, wondering how I got roped into this outing. At least Henry had my back and still wanted mac and cheese.

As I got into my driver's seat and drove the short distance to the main road, the woman on the phone dug her way into my mind. I had probably sounded a little too gruff.

And my cousin was right. She did sound gorgeous, but that didn't matter. What mattered was having kindness in a partner and the ability to see right from wrong. And obviously, I didn't know how to figure that out when dating women.

I gripped the steering wheel a little tighter as my mom popped into my head. I'd done a great job of keeping her out of my thoughts most of my life, so it was a shame she'd been so front and center lately, and this call didn't help matters any.

Sucking in a deep breath, I followed Lucas' car into the gravel parking lot. It had been a minute since I'd been to this place. It was propped on a cliff overlooking the water and was the size of a shoebox. I wasn't sure how a band and customers could actually fit inside at the same time.

I parked next to my cousin, and before I'd even turned off my car, he'd hopped out of his and rubbed his hands together as if he'd just ordered a full-pound rack of ribs. I chuckled to myself, knowing I'd be single for a long time.

"So, I'm not looking to find a wife tonight." Lucas eyed me with a smirk as I unbuckled Henry from his car seat and grabbed some books and toys to keep him occupied. "But you know, I'd love to find someone to connect with, maybe travel places with, and you know…just have a good time."

I smiled. "Ah, right. Simple as that. Snap your fingers, repeat your wish, and voila."

"Uncle Luke is silly," Henry chided.

"I think you're onto something." I glanced at my cousin. "You know, my son is highly gifted. He told me the same thing about ten minutes ago, and I think he's right."

Lucas bent over to Henry. "Just don't tell any of the ladies here that. Okay, little man?"

Henry's fingers wrapped around mine as we went into the restaurant.

We found a booth that faced an open garage door where the band was setting up on the deck.

"Nice." Lucas nodded, taking a sip. "This will be great for music and scoping."

Henry squeezed my hand before I lifted him into the booth as a bartender brought over a booster.

"What's Uncle Luke scoping?"

I laughed and thanked the bartender, who took our orders. "Sealife out in the water."

Lucas raised his brows up and down at a pair of ladies walking by, and I rolled my eyes.

When the bartender left, I leaned over and whispered, "You're making this a really cringy experience."

Lucas frowned. "I can't help that I'm attracted to women."

I glanced at Henry, who was flipping the pages of his picture book.

"So am I, but it's not like I have to have my tongue hanging out wagging."

Lucas took a sip of his beer and kicked his feet out the side of the booth. A breeze rolled in from outside, and I glanced over to see two women. One glanced over at us, cocked her head in confusion, and then frowned before tapping the woman in front of her, who wasn't turned in our direction. The mystery woman's dark hair cascaded down her back, and she wore a cute pair of worn jeans and a body-hugging red shirt. The two women could be sisters.

"What's caught your eye?" Lucas asked, surprised.

I shook my head. "Nothing."

He followed where my gaze just left and laughed. "Ah, nothing, huh?"

"You look a little tense there, buddy," Lucas chided.

"I'm fine." I looked down at the menu when I heard the women laughing. I picked up on a familiar tone and glanced over to see the one staring at me and the other, still turned away. But it was the one not looking that made every part of my body react. My gaze slid along her curvy body, and I held in a breath as her laughter drifted over.

"What's on the menu, Henry?" I leaned down to my son. "Want some fries and a burger?"

"Mm-hm."

"Good. Me too."

Another fit of laughs drifted over. There was something about the sound of her voice that was so calming and so…

Familiar.

Lucas shot me a wry grin. "Should I go introduce us to the lucky ladies or…"

"Seriously. You've gotta stop." I shook my head with a smile.

The place was getting busier, and the women's laughter was drowned out by a band plucking a few strings of a guitar and the tap of drums beating faintly as they checked the microphones.

When the bartender came back to take our orders, I

let out a sigh of relief. The sooner we ate, the quicker we could get out of here.

As I placed my order, the woman who'd been facing the other direction glanced over her shoulder, and my breath caught in my throat. She was gorgeous, but my chest tightened the moment she threw me a dirty look. Granted, it was kind of sexy, but it was no doubt a look of annoyance or anger or something.

"Why's she mad?" Henry asked, cupping his ears with his hands.

"Who?"

"The girl," Henry answered, pointing at the ladies when he removed his hands from his ears.

"Ah, she's not mad," I assured my three-year-old, but I wasn't so sure myself.

Lucas grinned as the two women stood. "Well, it looks like we might have company."

"Great," I muttered.

Within seconds, they were standing at the edge of our table with both of their arms crossed over their chests.

"Are you James Edwards?" the one asked, who wasn't the one I wanted to talk with.

"This is him. In. The. Flesh." My cousin nodded like a bobblehead. "Is there something we can help you with?"

"Yeah. I'd like to know why you're so rude and inconsiderate when all my sister wanted to do was return something to its rightful owner."

My eyes widened in surprise. "I have no idea what you're talking about."

The woman scowled at me, and the sister cocked her head, looking baffled and embarrassed.

Henry slid his hand to mine. "Daddy?"

The women didn't seem to notice that I had a short person next to me.

"The call earlier?" the woman pressed. "You hung up on her. My sister Amelia doesn't deserve that." She raised her hands, exasperated. "She took her evening off to ride all the way over here, and then you're rude."

"Oh, right." The sudden knots in my stomach tightened. "I apologize. Things are often more complicated than most know, but I do apologize."

Amelia. The name fit her so well. Her green eyes connected with mine, and I drew a breath. It would be my luck to be impolite to the one woman in the world who caught my attention.

"Amelia, I apologize. It was uncalled for to hang up on you, but I don't have anything to offer." I always wanted to set a good example for my son, and suddenly, things were taking a quick turn.

She scowled as her sister rolled her eyes. "I'm not trying to get anything from you. I don't *want* anything from you. I just wanted to return something that I think belongs to you, and don't worry about my sister Emily. She gets a little overprotective at times."

I shook my head, unsure of what she possibly had that I wanted.

She put her finger up in the air and smiled. "One sec."

"Where's she going?" Henry asked.

Amelia darted to her table, pulled something out of her large purse, and carried it over.

She set a stack of envelopes in front of me. "Are you JJ?"

"No." Henry shook his head. "His name's Daddy."

Lucas looked at me, reached over the table, and picked up my son instantly. He took him over to check out the instruments of the band.

"Yeah. Maybe for Jerky James." Her sister smiled, but the name shot through me like a lightning bolt. I hadn't heard anyone call me JJ since my mom.

Amelia scowled and elbowed her sister. "What? Are we suddenly twelve?"

"These belong to you," Amelia said softly, pushing

forward a stack of papers. "And I'm sorry about bleeding on them."

And before I could protest or tell them to take them back, the sisters spun on their heels and left the restaurant.

Lucas looked at me with surprise as he walked back with Henry, and I shook my head. "Don't say a word."

The band started playing as the pile of letters sat in front of me while I wondered in what cruel joke of a world would my mom leave me letters?

CHAPTER THREE

Amelia

"Well, that went well." Emily grimaced and let out a sigh. "It's funny how a man who's that easy on the eyes can be such a jerk."

I chuckled and nodded, thinking back to my sister's nickname for him. "But did you really have to call him Jerky James? And in front of his son?"

"You know how I freeze on stuff like that. It's all that came out and sounded halfway fitting." She grimaced. "And I somehow just saw red. I didn't even really think about the fact that he had his son with him or that he even had a son or is married."

"Right. It's typical for most people to rent children when they go out to eat because it always makes the event

37

more relaxing." I snickered and shook my head as the breeze from the ferry blew through my hair.

Our little island was coming into view, and I felt extremely antsy and wanted nothing more than to arrive back in my safe haven. The chain of islands off the coast was spectacular, and each had something to offer, but there was nothing better than arriving back at Curiosity Bay. It just screamed home. The ferry that went back and forth between the islands was smaller and carried more passengers than cars.

A chill went through me as the breeze picked up for nightfall. I'd promised my sister earlier that I'd grab a cup of tea with her tonight before we headed our separate ways until work tomorrow.

My only wish was that I could get Jerky James out of my head. There was something a little mysterious about him, and the emotion behind his gaze stirred something unsettling in me…a good unsettling.

And his little mini-me was pretty darn cute too, but none of that mattered. He was obviously with someone, or there'd be no little Jerky James.

"Who knew the kid you threw an apple at all those years ago at the orchard and made fall out of a tree would be so sexy all grown up."

I smiled, letting the sea air slide over my skin as I took

a deep breath. "Just my luck. And completely unavailable."

"It doesn't seem like he's changed much, either. What was it he did to deserve the apple to the forehead again?"

I hugged myself as a little chill fluttered through me again. It was funny. I kind of felt bad about it all of a sudden.

"He teased Mae about her braces." I smiled at my sister. "Do you think he knows I'm the one who did that all those years ago?"

Emily chuckled. "It didn't look like there was an ounce of recognition. Curiosity? Plenty. But no recognition."

My stomach swirled with her observation. "What do you mean, curiosity?"

She narrowed her eyes on me with a sharp, sisterly focus. "Why do you care?"

I shot my one shoulder up like I didn't really care and let out a sigh. "I don't. Just wondering what you meant by that because all I could gather from the exchange was that he didn't want to see me or the letters."

"I'm sure once he gets his head out of his butt, he'll be happy you went to all the trouble to give them to him."

I stared off toward our island and smiled, thinking back to how gorgeous JJ turned out to be. Not that it mattered. "I hope so, but I did what I thought was best, and that's all I can do."

My sister gave a quick nod. "Exactly."

She ran her fingers along the railing as the captain announced our arrival at Curiosity Bay. "He was pretty handsome if you're into the whole blue eyes and dark hair thing."

I wasn't about to confess that I was very much into that. "Well, I just need to figure out how to get the little book out of the vase, and then I'll put this entire ordeal behind me."

We made our way down the tiny stairwell with metal walls and tiny orange buoys in the shape of rings hanging within quick reach as a friendly reminder that if the ship goes down, you had better grab one and hope it floated.

We quickly descended the steps that led out to the walkway connecting to the dock. I adjusted the strap on my bag and sucked in a deep breath. I was really turning into a homebody, even though my home was a bit temporary until I found a new apartment to rent.

The island had everything I needed. There were tons of gift stores, restaurants, cafes, two grocery stores, a drug store, and anything and everything a tourist would want to do right at my fingertips. I could sign up for a seaplane excursion, go sea kayaking with a local guide, or even learn to make honey butter at one of the local farms. It was great. All things that sounded extremely fun to do one day when I had the time.

But until then, I was glad to be living here and working at the antique store.

"You're awfully quiet," Emily said, glancing over her shoulder.

I smiled and shrugged as we made our way up the small incline toward town. "Just thinking about how lucky I am to live here."

"Yeah. We really are. Did you still want to grab some tea, or is it too late?"

I could tell Emily really wanted to hang out, so I nodded. "Totally need something warm. Standing on the deck on the way over wasn't my brightest idea."

"Good."

We wound along the sidewalk to where Maddie's Tea Shop sprawled along the waterfront. This place was always a stop for tourists. The flagship store was located on Fireweed, but she'd managed to populate just about every island in the Northwest with her tea shops, and her flavors were addicting.

The moment we stepped inside, it was heaven. Vanilla, citrus, and something a little peppery drifted through the air. There was a small line of people waiting to get their loose teas, but we made our way over to the counter where we could order drinks.

And out of the blue, Jerky James invaded my

thoughts. It was as if his blue eyes were staring at me, but he wasn't here. I was safe. But I could just envision those piercing, beautiful, blue eyes.

This wasn't good.

Once I pulled out that little book from the vase, I'd have to send one of my sisters to drop it off or maybe mail it.

He wasn't a friendly person. That much was obvious, and I didn't need to get myself involved with someone who wasn't friendly.

Nice needed to be on the top of my must-have list, for once.

"My treat," Emily said, fanning her hand in front of me. "And it's your turn to order."

My cheeks reddened, and I quickly came up with the Snoozy Chami tea, which would hopefully do the trick when I got home.

As we took our cups of tea and sat down at a table overlooking the water, my sister caught a heavy sigh that escaped my lips.

"What's that all about?" she asked, quirking a brow.

"Nothing. I just…"

"Just what?"

"I thought he'd be thankful we brought him the letters. Instead, it was like he wished I'd just go away."

She shrugged and laughed. "Like I said, Jerky James."

"It's yet another reason I like to stay home after I'm done working. No dating game for me."

"Dating game?" Emily asked, taking a sip. "How did delivering something to James turn into thoughts of the dating world?"

I scowled. "That's not what I meant. I'm only trying to say that peopling is exhausting whether it's men or women, and I'm over it."

"Over it as in all of humanity?"

I chuckled and took a sip of chamomile tea. It soothed my throat, and soon it would help me drift to sleep…if I could just get James out of my head. "Yeah. Pretty much."

"Listen, I know you don't like to talk about stuff in the past, but what your BFF did to *you* was the worst of the worst, and what your fiancé did with *her* is unthinkable."

"Yet, here we are." I sighed and saw the ferry heading back to where it came from.

Right where James and his haunting eyes remained. I hid a chuckle and looked at my sister.

"I don't think you're over it," she announced.

I grinned, realizing she had no idea what I was really thinking about. "Oh, please. It's been years, and I'm totally over it."

"Since he didn't seem thrilled with what you delivered, are you going to worry about what's left in the vase?" Emily asked, finishing her tea.

"Remains to be seen. We still have eleven boxes left to unpack and two storage pods. Ask me when we're done. I honestly can't believe we scored so heavily on all that stuff. It's like they didn't even bother to look at it."

She nodded. "Maybe there's a reason James didn't care about what you gave him or any of the stuff. I mean, it looks like the company that we bought it from just went in and threw everything in boxes, we placed the highest bid, and voila."

I shrugged, feeling a nagging sensation settle in my stomach. "Maybe so."

"Hey, ladies. What are two sweet and sexy women doing drinking tea at this hour?"

My sister frowned and glanced over to see Bryce. He'd left Herman with a bowl of water out front.

"Just trying to relax before I head home," I told him as he eyed Emily.

"I don't understand why you never ask yours truly out for dinner, drinks, or bit of midnight fun." He laughed, scratching the scruff on his chin.

Bryce was actually a handsome guy, and he had a great sense of humor, except sometimes it was like he was a hot guy trapped in a ninety-year-old grandpa's dirty mind, which considering he'd stayed with his grandparents a lot growing up, made a bit of sense.

"Because I'm usually asleep by midnight, but what are you doing at this end of town?" I asked.

"I was actually just walking by and saw you two and thought I'd pop in." He scooted a chair to the table and took a seat.

Emily chuckled. "Okay."

"We were just talking shop," I explained. "We scored a big haul full of treasures, and we're nearly done sorting."

Bryce's brows rose, and he held up his hands and made the quote marks before talking. "When we're talking treasures, do we mean treasures or junk?"

Emily grinned. "In spite of Amelia's reputation, we actually made out on this deal. The items are really unique and quite valuable."

"A lot of them will be going to auction rather than sitting on our shelves," I added for emphasis.

"Interesting. I wonder who owned all the stuff." He glanced over at Herman outside, who was getting lots of pets.

"Not to be a downer, but isn't that kind of a liability?"

I glanced at the Doberman.

Bryce shook his head. "He's the sweetest dog in the world, and besides, he has no teeth. That was the one thing that deterred a lot of people at the adoption center, but it hasn't stopped him one bit from putting on the pounds."

I grinned, nodding. "Well, he is the sweetest dog I've met besides Dottie. The reputations of some breeds are so often blown out of proportion."

Bryce nodded in agreement.

Emily's smile turned into an odd grin. "We actually know whose belongings these were."

"Oh, really?" Bryce asked.

"Yup. Does James Edwards ring a bell?"

Bryce's jaw tightened. "As in *the* James Edwards, whose family has that fancy estate here they rarely visit?" A funny look covered his face. "Isn't that the kid who made fun of Mae, and you clocked him with his own apple?"

I chuckled. "Yeah. That's him."

Bryce laughed. "That was a fun day at the orchards. It's a shame the family doesn't open them up like they used to in the fall."

Emily nodded. "It was fun to go pick apples and drink hot cider. I did see someone pulling down that road last weekend, though."

Bryce nodded. "Well, you can never figure out what makes the rich tick."

"You think they're still well-to-do?" I asked, thinking back to James.

Bryce looked stunned. "Are you serious? They're like the most popular hard cider maker in the country. I think they've even gone off into other drinks."

I couldn't hide my surprise. "Seriously? I thought they just sold some timber and bottled apple juice."

"Back in the day, sure. But they got into the liquor business, and boom!"

"And he's cute." Emily wiggled her brows at me.

I rolled my eyes. "None of that stuff matters because he has a son and is obviously attached."

Emily nodded. "True. Plus, he was a total jerk."

Bryce laughed. "Well, he might have changed. Maybe he doesn't go around making fun of kids in braces anymore."

Emily shook her head. "No. He's still something else. Amelia tried delivering him some personal items from his mom, and he wanted nothing to do with her. He even hung up on her on the phone. We happened to bump into him when we were grabbing dinner, and he seemed as cold as a Yeti."

I frowned at her description. There was something

about him that made me feel a little…protective, which was completely bizarre. He could clearly protect himself, judging by the pounds upon pounds of muscle he'd put on over the years.

"He could have just been having a bad day," I offered.

Emily's brows rose. "Amelia, this is how you get yourself hurt. What you're experiencing is called red-flag syndrome. It means run as fast as you can. Don't pause and try to understand."

I snickered, knowing she was right. I always gave everyone the benefit of the doubt, and it came back and bit me in the bum when it came to my fiancé and best friend. "You made that term up."

She laughed. "It's a keeper."

"I think it's sweet that Amelia always tries to see the best," Bryce offered. "But I do think that your sister is right. Don't start getting curious about what makes the grumpy man tick. I'm a man, and I'm not grumpy. We're not all that way, and I've been told by a lot of people that I'm a catch."

Emily chuckled. "Your grandma doesn't count."

"Yeah, she does." Bryce laughed and stood. "On that note, I'm going to go home and lick my wounds."

When he left, my sister leaned forward. "You're not actually thinking about James, are you?"

"What makes you think that?"

"Let's see, the right half of your mouth curls up for no reason as you stare off into the distance. Your eyes dance a little when we bring up you nailing the kid with the apple. And you didn't even notice that I drank the rest of your tea."

I smiled and shook my head. "I've told you a million times. I'm over trying to find Mr. Perfect or Mr. Right."

"That's what worries me," Emily muttered. "What if you're aiming for Mr. Wrong again?"

I nodded. "I've obviously fallen for Mr. Wrong more times than I'd like to admit. What I meant was that I'm over trying to date men. Period. No matter what, who, or where they are. My sole focus is the antique store. Not dating. Not relationships. Not any of it. It's not like Mom and Dad are getting any younger. I want them to see what we can do and feel like they can finally retire."

And I wished with every part of my being that what I just said was completely true, but I couldn't stop thinking about what made James look so troubled by the letters I'd shoved in front of him. I wasn't trying to date him. I merely wanted to make sure he was okay.

"Amelia, just a quick FYI."

I looked up at my sister.

"You're a horrible liar. Just make sure to bring me

with you if you decide to take him the damn vase with the diary inside."

CHAPTER FOUR

James

The letters taunted me. What I should do is run them through the paper shredder without reading them, but for some reason, I just wanted to torture myself. But I think it had more to do with the woman who went to all the effort to bring them to me than it did with actually wanting to read what was inside.

From my mother.

The woman who abandoned me.

Couldn't be bothered with me.

And then I'd managed to find a woman who did the same thing to her own son.

My little Henry.

He was so helpless. How could someone do that?

I let out a sigh and walked over to my desk. Last night after my cousin struck out yet again at the bar, I came home and set the stack of letters on the desk in my office, played with Henry, and went to bed.

But since I woke up, I couldn't stop thinking about the woman who tracked me down and wanted me to have them. It wasn't her fault she didn't know I had zero interest in any of it. I didn't care how much money I gave away by calling some outfit to deal with all my mom's belongings. I just didn't want anything to do with any of my past.

When I think of my childhood, happy memories wash through me because of my grandparents and cousins, not my parents. I never even knew my dad.

And then, once everything happened with Henry's mother, I was one hundred percent broken. Not for me, but for my son. I never in a million years thought I'd be attracted to someone who could do that to her own son.

Henry deserved to have a mother and a father who loved him and supported him.

I was grateful for Mary, to say the least.

Amelia wouldn't know any of that. She was just trying to do something nice. It was what people did on these small islands. And then I was a complete jerk about it.

But in my defense, over the years, I'd been used and

abused for who my family was more times than not. That was probably what happened with Henry's mom too, and I just didn't see it coming.

Even my best friends back in school only wanted to hang out because of our pool and the trips they got to tag along on. That was probably why my cousin and I were such good friends. We wanted nothing from one another other than friendship.

I let out a sigh and stood at my window overlooking the gardens that stretched to the shoreline. This place gave me the perfect escape from it all. Once I drove through the gates, I didn't have to worry about any of the negativity or problems.

But those were my issues, not Amelia's. She wouldn't know that ten out of ten females I'd dated were after my last name and money. She wouldn't know that my mom decided I was more trouble than I was worth at age seven. She wouldn't know that the one and only place I could decompress was behind gates on one side and bordered by water on the other.

She wouldn't know that I was that messed up, and only my son held me together.

The least I could do was offer her an apology.

I shook my head and wandered down a couple of hallways and through the family room until I reached the kitchen and opened the fridge to pull out a soda. I cracked it open and took a sip as I stared at the label.

A smile touched my lips as I thought back to my grandfather when I told him I'd had a brilliant idea to expand our beverage line to include alcohol. I was in my mid-twenties. He thought I was crazy. Actually, I think he used the word insane. But regardless, he trusted my vision, and the hard cider took off immediately. I was probably more surprised than my grandfather when it sold more than our regular lines of apple juice.

But what made me the happiest was that he and my grandma lived long enough to see my vision come alive. We'd managed to expand into flavored ciders as well. By the time I was in my early thirties, the company continued to thrive, and my uncle and cousins were extremely grateful since it's a family business.

I took another swig of the soda and walked over to the French doors that led onto the patio. The warm breeze ruffled the line of boxwood surrounding this portion of the patio. I just wished they would have been around to watch Henry grow up.

My phone buzzed, and I noticed my cousin's grinning mug pop up on the screen.

"Hey, Lucas. What's up?" I sat on a bench and kicked my feet out in front of me.

"Are you outside? Why aren't you at the office?"

I laughed. "I have a doctor's appointment later and took the day off, and your parents decided to take Henry to the zoo, so I thought I'd buy myself a little quiet time before I head to the doc. Are you going to rat me out?"

Lucas chuckled. "Since this is probably the first time you've taken time off in ten years, I'll keep it to myself. Do you remember those women from last night?"

How could I forget?

"Yeah. What about them?"

He was silent for a few beats and finally spoke. "Do you think since they hate you that they hate me by association?"

I scowled and looked toward the water. "Who says they hate me?"

"Seriously? Was this a surprise? Should I act like I didn't notice them hightailing it out of there after they dealt with you?"

I groaned and hung my head in my hands. "So, I was even worse than I remembered?"

"Are we just talking about at the bar or back to when you didn't call Amelia back and then hung up on her?"

"I feel bad about that."

"You should."

"Thanks for that."

"Someone's gotta tell you the truth. You're surrounded by people you pay well and who will lie to you to keep the paychecks coming."

His words stunned me. I hadn't really thought about it much, but I suppose he had a point.

"So, why did you want to reach out to them?"

"I thought the one who called you Jerky James was cute."

I laughed and shook my head. "Of course you did."

Relief spread through me when I realized he wasn't interested in Amelia.

Not that it mattered. I'd pretty much ruined our first impression.

"I was planning on sending flowers to the place Amelia works as an apology. At least wait until they're delivered."

"How do you know where she works?"

I bit my lip and sat back up, hoping I didn't sound too pathetic. "I just did a reverse lookup from the number she called from the first time my assistant gave the message to me. The second must have been from her cell when she was already on the island."

"I see."

"What?"

"Nothing. Just curious."

"About what?"

"Why you care."

"What's that supposed to mean?" I scratched my jawline, feeling the morning scruff and remembering I forgot to shave.

"This normally wouldn't phase you, especially since you had no interest in what was delivered, which leads me to believe you have an interest in who delivered it. I think you've got a thing for Amelia. That was her name, right?"

"You're sounding like your mom." I laughed. "Will you start wearing high heels like Aunt Nancy next? And yeah. Her name is Amelia."

"Normal James wouldn't remember any woman's name."

I laughed and shook my head. Lucas was really starting to sound like his mom. She was constantly pestering both of us about finding a woman and settling down. If Lucas even dared to mention a female's name, his mother was calling a wedding planner.

"It wasn't a normal day. I don't generally get accosted with a handful of letters from my deceased mom and get called a name in front of my son."

Lucas laughed. "Ouch. Okay. Fine. Maybe you don't have the hots for her. Maybe I'll ask her out instead."

It suddenly felt like I had indigestion, and I had to chuckle. "Fine. You win. She's intriguing."

"So, she's off limits."

"Very."

"Okay, just let me know when the coast is clear, and I'll try to figure out how to contact the feisty one."

I thought about whether I wanted to be nice to my cousin or not. I did some quick research this morning and saw that the antique store was family-owned, and all of Amelia's siblings were involved, along with her parents. He could just call the number I had.

"Okay. I'll let you know when I send the flowers."

"Hey, is everything okay? You know, with going to the doctor and everything?"

"Totally fine."

"Okay. Peace out," Lucas told me.

I laughed and ended the call, but my mind kept veering to Amelia. I'd lived up to her sister's nickname for me, and I hoped I could at least make amends.

Rolling up my shirtsleeves to look on my phone for a florist, I thought about my day. My cousin was right. I rarely took time off. Maybe I should take a trip to Marigold Island after my doctor's appointment. I hadn't been to my grandparents' estate in a long time. I could check it out, wander the property, and maybe grab some dinner in town before heading back here.

As I entered the flower order online for Amelia, I was stumped at how much to spend. It wasn't like I sent apology flowers every day. Shoot. I didn't send flowers period. Was a hundred bucks enough? Too little? It didn't seem like you'd get many for that. I entered three hundred, filled out the card message, and submitted my order.

Hopefully, after these flowers, if she ever bumped into me again, she wouldn't run the other way.

CHAPTER FIVE

Amelia

"Alright. Who's hiding a boyfriend?" my mom asked as a deliveryman brought in an enormous, and I mean enormous, floral arrangement. The guy could barely fit through the door before struggling through the rest of the store with the arrangement swaying and bowing with each step. I kept one eye open as he made his way through the aisles.

"Where should I put this?" he mumbled through the red roses and blue delphinium.

My mom laughed. "It won't fit on the counter."

"Maybe here on this dining table," I offered.

The man grunted as he carefully slid the arrangement onto the large table and took a step back with a drip of sweat running down his forehead.

"I didn't think I was going to make it. Our funeral arrangements aren't even that huge."

Chuckling, I took in the gorgeous flowers. I think there was every kind of flower imaginable tucked into the arrangement.

The man turned around and waved to my mom. "Have a good day."

"Well, nobody died, so who are they from?" my mom asked, coming around the counter toward the table.

I shrugged, looking for a card. "I bet they're for Audrey. She had that date the other night."

My mom's eyes lit up. "If that's the case, she'd better snag this man. This floral arrangement isn't cheap, and it's beyond thoughtful. I mean, who sends flowers nowadays? Nobody does this anymore. It's a shame, though."

I nodded in agreement as I thought back to my last relationship. My mom had a point. There wasn't one time that my fiancé sent me flowers or brought them to me, not even a weed from the garden. I would have been thrilled if he'd even bent over and snapped a dandelion off for me because at least then I'd know he remembered I existed. Suddenly, I wondered if he had ever brought my best friend flowers.

Probably.

"Come on. Where's the card?" my mom prodded.

"Go get Audrey," I mumbled.

"They're for her?"

I shrugged. "I'm assuming."

My mom eyed me and chuckled. "You know what they say about assuming."

Right when she said that, I found the tiny envelope and was floored to see my name on it.

"There must be a mistake." I glanced at my mom. "I don't know anyone."

Dottie snorted at the door to go outside, and my mom straightened. "Oh, Dottie. You have the worst timing. Duty calls."

I chuckled. "No pun intended, I'm sure."

My mom smiled and shook her head. "Hurry. Open the thing."

I slid my finger under the flap and tugged on the small card as she went outside with the pug.

Amelia,

I apologize from the bottom of my heart. I never intended to be Jerky James. I hope all is forgiven, and I appreciate the time and effort it took to deliver my mom's letters.

Warm Wishes,

James Edwards

I froze. My lips turned to parchment paper, and my tongue felt like it was swelling twice the size. I quickly slid the card back into the envelope and stared at the flowers as I tried to come up with an excuse.

James.

The guy I'd been trying to forget about since I found letters addressed to JJ, since he hung up on me, since I finally saw him in the bar. The guy who was clearly not interested in kindness.

And the guy who was obviously attached with child.

I scowled and shoved the envelope into my back pocket.

"Who're they from?" my mom asked after returning with Dottie. She bent over and unhooked the leash, and Dottie wandered to under the dining table and sat down with a thud and a snort.

"A client."

My mom's brows rose. "A client?"

She looked around the overstuffed store. "One that we currently have?"

I bit my bottom lip, and my cheeks reddened as Emily

wandered over from upstairs.

"Oh, wow. Lucas was right. That's a humdinger of an arrangement." Emily wiggled her brows and eyed my mom and me. "Well, is all forgiven?"

My mom pursed her lips together as they formed into a smile, and I attempted to avoid all eye contact.

"Forgiven?" my mom prompted.

I looked over at my sister. "Lucas? Who's Lucas?"

"That was James' cousin last night. You know, the cute guy James was with? He just called." She looked exasperated. "And asked me out."

"Oh, wow. Okay." I turned to the flowers and scratched my head.

"Okay, I'm over here dying to know who James and Lucas are." My mom waved her hand in front of my face.

"Do you want to tell her the JJ saga or should I?" my sister asked.

I chuckled and shrugged. "You go ahead. I have some stuff to take care of."

And I did. There was a pile of items on my desk that needed pricing before they came out onto the floor. They were still from the Edwards lot, nothing that needed to go to auction, but still really beautiful items, mostly jewelry.

As I trudged up the stairs, I glanced over my shoulder

at the flowers, and they took my breath away. To say they were impressive was an understatement. I swore I almost had heart-shaped pupils when I read the notecard. But that wasn't how I operated any longer. I wasn't easily swept off my feet.

Right?

Then why was I still staring at the flowers over my shoulder?

I took the next step, only to find that my left foot developed a sudden case of rebelliousness. My foot took a sidestep, causing me to stumble forward. I turned my attention back to the stairs in front of me, but it was too late. In a desperate attempt to regain my balance, my arms flailed like a wild flamingo as I performed an impromptu pirouette before my body crashed onto the wooden stairs.

My sister and mom gasped, but it was all a blur because gravity was not done with me. She seized the moment and spiraled me down the stairs with a thud.

I was afraid to move. Nothing could end well with a tumble like that when a person was in her thirties.

"I'm calling 9-1-1," my mom yelped. "Can you move? Can you blink?"

All I saw was Dottie rushing over before a tongue smacked my cheek and eyeball, licking me endlessly.

I chuckled as Emily knelt down beside me. "Are you

dead?"

"Not yet," I groaned as Dottie's big, fat tongue came for my eyeball again.

"Let me help you up."

"Don't touch her. The 9-1-1 operator says to leave her like she is until the medics get here."

"Please don't," I hissed at my sister.

Dottie stopped licking me. Instead, she jumped on my back and nestled into a tight circle.

"Does that hurt?" my mom asked as she stayed on the phone with the operator.

"No. The pug on me isn't the main issue, Mom."

My older sister Mae wandered in, and her eyes turned to saucers. "What happened? Is Dottie okay? Did she get squashed?"

I laughed, afraid to move since my mom was pacing back and forth steps away from me. "Don't worry about me. I'm totally fine down here."

Mae scanned my contorted body and shook her head. "Seriously. What on earth happened?"

"I glanced back at the flowers on the table, and I took a tumble down the stairs."

Mae's gaze brightened. "You got flowers? Where?"

"They're from James Edwards," Emily informed her.

"The kid who made fun of my braces and you took him out with an apple?" Mae nodded in approval. "He's done well for himself. They're beautiful flowers."

"I'm glad your priorities are straight, but he's not single," I mumbled. "Now, if you don't mind, can one of you get Dottie off so that I can stand, please?"

My mom scowled. "No, you can't stand. The operator said you need to remain still."

Ignoring my mom, Mae lifted Dottie off my back, and Emily reached for my hand to help me up.

"You don't know that he's not single," Emily corrected.

Sirens echoed down the street just as I stood and hissed in pain.

"See?" My mom shook her head. "Put her back down."

"I'm already up," I protested, keeping my foot in the air.

In under a minute, the sirens blared through the front of our antique store, and two men and one woman came barging in.

And of course, I recognized all three. I'd grown up with the two guys and the woman had married a family friend a few years back.

The questions came pouring out. Did you hit your head? Does your neck hurt? Your back? Can you put pressure on your foot?

I touched my head gently as a minor ache thumped at the base of my head.

"Your head hurts?" Leslie, the female medic, asked.

I nodded slowly, and she snapped her fingers. The two male medics, Jim and Larry, left the building and returned with a stretcher.

"No, I'm okay." I shook my head, which only made it worse. "I'll have one of my sisters take me to the doctor."

"You can't walk, and your head hurts." Mae scowled. "Don't be stubborn."

On cue, the two men rolled up with the stretcher. I pressed my lips together in protest but let them help me on the gurney. A sharp pain shot down my ankle and through my foot as I adjusted myself.

"The entire town is going to see," I muttered more to myself than anyone.

"Just wear this." Emily unfolded a white sheet and laid it over me like I'd died.

"This is making it so much worse," I mumbled through the fabric.

Emily laughed. "You can't have it both ways. Either

you don't want to be seen or you do."

I groaned into the sheet as I kept my eyes open and stared at the white cotton percale resting on my forehead.

The medics started pushing through the antique store as my head ached more, but I was pretty sure it wasn't because of the fall.

"Oh, beautiful flowers," Leslie said.

"I think my daughter has an admirer," my mom said.

"With that many flowers, I'd say he's about to get down on one knee."

Mortification shot through me. "It's not like that at all. Just a misunderstanding," I spoke through the sheet.

They rolled me through the door, and I heard a crowd of gasps on the sidewalk as Dottie started barking.

"Is everything okay?" Bryce rushed over to the mound of a sheet on the gurney. "Is she...Is Amelia..."

I chuckled and raised my arm as Bryce shrieked ten octaves higher. "She's not dead."

"Of course, I'm not dead." I pulled the sheet down from my face and saw Bryce's extremely pale face as he eyed my sisters and mom. "The whole town is talking about the accident. They heard one of the Evans sisters fell down the stairs and broke her neck. I knew it had to be you because you can't even stand upright on flat surfaces." I scowled as the medics kept rolling me toward the ambulance.

"She didn't break her neck. Maybe her foot, but…" Mae eyed me with a half-crooked grin. "Who knew you could become so popular by falling?"

"Excuse me," a man's voice I vaguely recognized drifted through the air. "Is everything okay? Is Amelia…"

My eyes widened, and I shot up as the medics lifted me into the ambulance. I smacked my face on a metal contraption of some sort when my gaze met James'.

"Amelia." He rushed to the opening of the ambulance as the driver glanced behind him. Two of the medics took a seat next to me, and Leslie sat up front.

"Only one passenger can go with you," she explained.

My sisters and mom all took a few steps back, and the next thing I knew, the two medics pulled James into the cab and shut the doors with a thud and off we went.

CHAPTER SIX

James

No one should look ravishing on a stretcher in an ambulance. It defied all logic. But Amelia looked incredible and…quite possibly annoyed.

The ambulance jolted forward, and our eyes connected. I noticed a red tint cascade across her cheeks before she looked away.

"It takes a special kind of talent to look this fabulous while being rushed to a hospital," one of the medics told Amelia. "I see a lot of women strapped down here, and none of them have looked as pleasant as you."

I scowled and turned to look at the guy. He had a flirty grin on his face, and Amelia rolled her eyes.

"Isn't it like against the Hippocratic Oath or

something to flirt with a patient?" she asked.

The guy laughed. "I'm not a doctor, but all I'm saying is that you're a really pretty accident victim."

"You're only saying that because you've known me since I was ten, and you learned I could land a good punch."

The guy nodded.

She looked over at me, and I couldn't help but smile. "I'm sure it's completely inappropriate, but I have to agree. You look fantastic for someone who catapulted down some stairs."

She frowned and rubbed her head. "How'd you hear about it?"

"I was grabbing some lunch down the road, and that guy you scared half to death told the entire café. Apparently, he has some scanner for the island on his cellphone."

Her eyes sparkled with an intensity that made me wish I'd never hung up on her. There was something about her that just screamed to my soul, and I wasn't even sure I'd had one recently.

Amelia chuckled, and the melodious sound bounced around the small cab as the other medic took some vitals. "That explains why he always knows everything about everything. This small-town living is something else."

Her eyes stayed on mine a beat too long, and I felt the

electricity run through us. There was no way it could be in my mind.

Right?

Or maybe she was delirious from her head injury.

"Thank you for the flowers." The corner of her lip turned up.

I straightened and glanced around the ambulance. Leslie had her head craned to see us all from the front passenger seat as the sirens blared.

"It's the least I could do."

"Ooh, so you're the boyfriend. Either you're in the doghouse or you're about to drop down on one knee," the female paramedic gushed.

Amelia clamped her eyes shut in embarrassment. "Not the case. Neither scenario is reality. But thank you."

There was something about Amelia's reaction that I absolutely loved. I couldn't tear my eyes away from her. I shouldn't want to see her mortified, but it was so damn cute the way the small wrinkles formed along the corner of her eyes and her nose scrunched up in protest.

"ETA two minutes," the driver warned.

The two medics began getting her ready, and I snuck another look in her direction, but she was already watching me.

"What are you doing on my island?" Her brow curled slightly, and I detected a hint of snark.

I laughed. "Your island? I didn't know it was yours."

She smirked. "You know what I mean."

"I was planning on stopping by our family's property, but I wanted to grab some lunch first."

Amelia almost looked a tad disappointed, and I wasn't sure why. "Do you spend much time here?"

I shook my head. "No. I haven't been here for a while. My cousins and aunt and uncle get a lot more use than I do."

"Oh." She nodded. "That's too bad."

"Arrived," the driver called back as we rolled to a quick stop. The sirens went silent and Amelia glanced at me.

The two medics popped open the doors and rolled Amelia out with a clang. I hopped out, following behind as they made their way into the emergency room where the doctor and several nurses were waiting.

"Hello there, Amelia," the older male physician greeted her.

"Hey, Uncle Stan," she said with a sigh. "I told Mom this was completely unnecessary."

"A head injury is nothing to be trifled with." He glanced at me. "And who's this?"

The medics went over to the nurse's station to do

paperwork as I stared at Amelia. Her uncle had a good question. At the moment, I felt like some jerk of a guy who was trying everything in my power to wipe the slate clean. I had no business riding in the ambulance with her and certainly none as they wheeled her into a room and closed the curtains.

"He's just a friend."

"With bad timing," I added.

Her gaze fluttered to mine, and that familiar charge ran through me. Wherever she was, I wanted to be. Even if that meant in a hospital room.

Doctor Stan didn't pay any attention and started asking Amelia a million questions about her fall as three women slid the curtain aside and dashed in with a rush. They were the same women who'd stepped back and let me get pulled into the ambulance. I recognized one of them from the night Amelia handed over the stack of letters from my mom and nicknamed me Jerky James. It was her sister and the one my cousin apparently decided was his destiny.

A smile touched my lips as her sister's eyes focused razor-thin on me. It was like a challenge she was throwing in my direction, but I had no idea what the test was.

Yet, for some strange reason, I wanted to accept.

"We'll be running some tests, but so far, things look like we're okay." The doctor shook his head and glanced over at the group of women. "What did she do this time?" He handed her a gown. "Put this on."

The older one chuckled and shook her head. "She was busy admiring a big bouquet of flowers that arrived for her. She was going up the stairs, glanced over her shoulder, and the rest is history. You know, she's never gotten flowers. Not even from her fiancé."

"Mom," Emily chirped, squeezing her arm.

Okay, so that was Amelia's mother. But I felt a scowl lower on my mouth, not realizing Amelia had a fiancé. That changed things. I hadn't noticed a ring, but maybe she didn't wear it.

A little gasp spilled from Amelia's lips, and I looked over to see her bright red complexion while she gave her mom a death stare and her sisters held in a chuckle.

And then it dawned on me. She was in the hospital because of me. My flowers. This was why I didn't people. Havoc always ensued.

I cleared my throat, and my eyes fell to the gown Amelia was holding. "I should probably get going."

"You don't have to leave," Emily spat out, shaking her head.

"You don't have to stay." Amelia smiled, reaching out to touch my arm.

The jolt from her touch surprised me, but I didn't move.

"I don't want to intrude." I shook my head. "But I had planned on stopping by the shop to tell you thank you for going to all that trouble to deliver those things from my mom. It was very kind of you, and you really didn't deserve being hung up on either. I apologize." I rocked on my heels and drew a breath. "I wish you a speedy recovery."

A man who looked eerily similar to the rest of the women standing in the room darted through the curtain, getting tangled in the meantime.

"I heard Amelia's here after falling down the stairs again." His icy green eyes stumbled upon me, and he immediately scowled. "Who are you?"

"He's the guy who caused her to fall down the stairs, Brad," Emily chided.

In an instant, *Brad* came toe-to-toe with me, but I was a couple of inches taller. It was safe to say Emily was the troublemaker of the family.

"Enough, Brad. Or should I call you Thor?" Amelia's voice teased. "He sent me flowers, and I tripped on my own two feet admiring them."

I stuck my hand out. "Brad, is it?"

He nodded, and I felt his firm grip. I made sure to

make mine firmer.

"Good to meet you," I said calmly, looking at the exit. I only needed to make it a few more feet, and I'd finally be able to breathe.

Brad let go of my hand and glanced at the women. "Is he your boyfriend or something?"

Oh, not again.

I shoved my hand through my hair and shook my head. "But I should be going. Amelia, thank you again."

I shoved the curtain aside and felt my heart racing as I strode out of the room, nearly bumping into the tech who was ready to wheel Amelia away for a CT scan once she changed.

"Hey, wait a second," Brad's voice called from behind.

I spun around while he snapped his fingers. "You're that Edwards kid who Amelia nailed with an apple all those years ago." He snapped his fingers again. "You made fun of Mae's braces."

No way.

That was Amelia?

I didn't recognize her in the least bit, but I suppose people changed a bit from age seven to our thirties.

"What? You didn't know?" He laughed.

I scratched my chin and smiled. I'd always wondered why I'd gotten a raised lump from some random girl at my grandparents' apple farm, but I did remember the events a little differently.

"Well, see ya around." I waved and made my way down the hall as I heard Amelia chatting away with the tech wheeling her away.

As I walked out the automatic doors, it suddenly hit me that I rode here in an ambulance and had no way to get back to my car unless I wanted to walk or wait for a ride-share. I pulled up the app and glanced at the wait time, which was insane, but it made sense, considering we were on an island in the middle of nowhere.

So, walking it would be.

CHAPTER SEVEN

Amelia

I couldn't get James out of my head. The way he snuck glances at me or how his smile lifted higher when I spoke, and I loved that he didn't bow down to my brother.

This wasn't good. Not good at all. I should not be interested in a guy who is arrogant, rude, and completely out of touch with reality.

"You're all clear, Amelia. Your head is as good as it'll ever get, but you need to keep your foot up for the next few days with ice. It's a mild sprain. No antique store."

"I knew I was fine," I said, scooting off the hospital bed.

My brother laughed and shook his head. "I really think we need to sign you up for tumbling classes so you learn how to fall better."

I laughed as my uncle nodded in agreement.

"So, who was that fellow here with you?" my uncle asked with a twinkle in his eyes. He was my mother's brother, and he never liked my previous fiancé or any other guy I'd brought around.

"Just an acquaintance."

"Who sends flowers?" He smiled and shrugged as he logged off the computer in the emergency room.

"I just know him from work, and there was a simple misunderstanding." I pulled my shirt over my head and slid my arms out of the gown while keeping it up before tugging my shirt down.

Sliding off the bed with my feet and finding the leg holes of my jeans, I pulled them up and tossed the gown on the bed.

"See you on the second Sunday for dinner at our house," Uncle Stan said, giving a wave before heading out the door.

"Just an acquaintance?" My brother grumbled a laugh. "Men don't stare at their friends like the way he looked at you."

A tingling sensation fluttered through me. Maybe James' casting an extra couple of looks my way didn't mean

I was losing my mind.

"Well, we have nothing in common, apart from his taste in flowers, and that selection could have been left up to the florist." I shrugged. "I have too much going on in life to care."

I tried to make my tone half sigh and half floaty for extra effect.

"You're telling me every time you glanced at him and got that funny look in your eyes was all because of flowers?"

We wheeled past the nurse's station in the wheelchair toward the double doors to the parking lot.

"That's precisely what I'm saying. Besides, we're from very different worlds."

"How so?" My brother opened the passenger door on his Audi, and I plopped down on the leather seat and strapped in.

"He's some rich guy who can give away priceless heirlooms at a discount just so he's not bothered with having to get his hands a little dirty."

My brother laughed and shook his head before shutting my door and taking the wheelchair back to the hospital before walking around to get into the driver's seat.

He started the car and slowly pulled out of the parking lot as I thought about James. There was some odd connection between us. I could feel it, and on some weird level, I think I felt it when I threw an apple at him all those years ago. It was like he annoyed me so much, I just wanted to bug him more.

A sigh slipped from my lips, and my brother glanced in my direction with a raised brow.

I scowled. "What?"

"Whatcha thinking about?"

"Nothing. Okay, fine. Men and how I'm always drawn to the wrong ones."

A few seconds of silence rested between us.

"I'll be the first to admit that you've had some pretty epic dating fails in the past. Remember that time you went on a blind date and wound up at a funeral?"

"It was only a memorial service." I groaned and slid slightly in my seat. "And there is zippo reason to bring that up again. It's never happened since."

Brad burst into laughter. "Yeah, I hope not. I doubt the odds of that happening to anyone is like one in a zillion."

"Are you trying to make me feel better or worse about my dating life?"

"Come on, Sis."

"It was horrific." I stared straight ahead, willing the smile to stay away from my lips. "I don't need to be reminded that my dating life is full of trauma."

"I still can't believe you stayed instead of making a quick exit."

I finally couldn't resist the smile that sprang onto my lips. "It was so awful. I felt horrible, and then when I finally snuck away and made it to the correct address, my blind date was pissed." I shook my head. "The guy ranted and raved about me being a liar." I shivered at the memory of the guy.

Brad shook his head. "It was good you found out early that the guy had anger issues."

"That's one way of looking at it." I glanced at the ink-blue water rippling in the distance, and the color instantly reminded me of James.

Darn it.

"You're a magnet for chaos."

"It's a gift." I chuckled and leaned my head on the window. "And dating isn't simple."

Brad groaned and shook his head. "That's the problem, Amelia. Dating isn't supposed to be hard, either."

"Oh, please. If it's not hard, why is my favorite brother still single? I mean, I've had my fair share of dating fiascos, but at least I've never accidentally set someone's hair on fire during a romantic candlelit dinner."

He grimaced and nodded. "How would I know she'd use that much hair product? The candles were like a foot away from where we were sitting. It still worked out, though."

"By nearly setting her hair ablaze? Yes, please show me the ways of dating. You're obviously more gifted than me," I retorted, giggling.

"Fine. Maybe it's safe to say that dating disasters run in the family," Brad said, nudging me playfully in the knee.

I leaned back, and a memory popped right in. "Oh, my gosh. You know what's even worse?"

Closing my eyes, I couldn't stop laughing. "Remember that time I accidentally went out on a date with my ex-boyfriend's twin brother? I couldn't tell them apart, and he was all too eager to let it play out. If it weren't for you being at home and running into my actual boyfriend and taking him to the pizza parlor, I don't know what could have happened."

"And that was back in high school."

I groaned. "I'm doomed."

"We're all doomed," Brad said, turning down the road to my tiny and very temporary apartment. "Mom and Dad set the bar too high."

I turned in my seat. "You think that's it? That's the problem?"

He shrugged. "It's the only thing I can think of."

Brad chuckled, pulling in front of my turquoise door.

"I'll take it so I don't feel so bad about all the other horrible dates you don't know about." I unbuckled, and my brother was already around the car helping me out when I shook my head. "Maybe it's also that I have a brother who's always there for me."

Brad laughed. "I don't have much choice when I have a sister like you. I'm almost afraid to leave you alone."

I rolled my eyes and glanced across the street to see a bunch of tourists congregating at the ice cream shop. It was one of the downsides of this apartment. I had zero willpower and already had a ton of excuses to stop by for lunch or dinner.

The warm air felt wonderful after being turned into an icicle at the hospital, but I almost didn't want to go into my apartment. It wasn't home. My other apartment had been my home for years, and here, I just felt like a stranger in a box, afraid to do anything to make it mine, but I should at least try. I'd probably be here for at least a few months.

Brad opened the front door for me and led me to the couch. It wasn't my couch. The place came furnished. There were some navy curtains framing a window that overlooked the ocean if you stood on the tips of your toes, tilted your head to the left just perfectly, and did a little hop.

The kitchen cabinets had been painted navy, and the brushstrokes could be seen across the room, along with the cracks in the Formica. If you turned in the other direction, you could see a lumpy bed tucked in the corner. There was nothing inviting about this place.

My brother flipped on a few lights and got me settled with the remote and a blanket that actually was mine. My family somehow brought home the gigantic arrangement from James and placed it on the coffee table before I got home from the hospital. That was about the only thing that brought life to my dinky place. Seeing it brought a sloppy grin to my face that I knew I had to hide from my brother.

Brad wandered over to the kitchen, pulled some ice out of the freezer, and filled a bag before coming back and handing it over for my foot.

"Thanks for doing all this, best big brother in the world." I grinned at him and batted my lashes.

"Okay. What else do you want?"

"Ice cream for dinner."

He smirked. "From across the street?"

I nodded with an even wider grin.

"Fine. What kind?"

"Surprise me."

He laughed and turned around, only taking a few steps to get out of my tiny apartment.

I turned on the television and fielded some texts from

my sisters wanting to know if I'd made it home yet and noticed the flowers.

My faint doorbell dinged into the room, and I practically leaped off the couch, rushing over for my ice cream.

But the moment I opened the door to see my brother and the ice cream delivery, my mouth dropped open. I didn't know what to say or do. As I stood staring, my phone buzzed with a text from my brother. I didn't bother reading it since whatever he wanted to tell me was standing at my door.

I took a deep breath to compose myself as James stared at me with a lopsided grin and two scoops of black cherry ice cream. He was the most gorgeous person I'd ever seen. It didn't matter what he was doing. The guy just always managed to make my heart skip a few beats.

But he was attached.

"I bumped into your brother at the shop, and he said he was taking you ice cream, and I volunteered to bring it over once he said you were right across the street."

I bit my bottom lip and watched him.

"And full transparency. He gave me your cell number too."

My mouth still hung open as I kept my weight off my bad foot.

My heart fluttered as I tried to form a coherent thought, let alone a sentence. "Um, h–hi, James. Thanks for delivering the ice cream. Aren't you married?"

"You're welcome, and no." He smiled. "I'm not married." James handed me the cone, and his fingers gently brushed against mine.

A jolt of excitement surged through me.

"Oh." This news nearly made me faint. I'd already put him in the no-zone, and now he was in the go-zone.

Red flags.

Red flags.

His eyes focused on me. "Does ice cream usually do this to you?"

"Yes." I laughed and shook my head. "Okay, no. I was just expecting my brother."

James' smile only widened, and he pointed behind him. "I can go grab him if you'd like. He sat down at a bench with some of his own."

I chuckled and took a lick of the ice cream. "No, this is a nice change."

"What did your uncle-slash-doctor say about the fall?" he asked, not taking his eyes off me.

"He said my head is as good as it will ever be, and I just have a light sprain." I smiled, thinking back to my family.

"Which I knew, but my mom panicked and called 9-1-1, and my sisters were no help in convincing her otherwise."

"You have a tight family." It was more of a statement than a question, but I nodded.

"We do. It's a blessing and a curse." I took another lick. "What about you?"

He shook his head, and I saw that same unusual look dart through his gaze. "No, my grandparents raised me, and they've since passed. I'm really close with my cousin and his family, but probably not quite the same. If it weren't for my son…" His voice trailed off and he shrugged.

And that very feeling I had the first night I'd met him dug deep into my soul.

"So, this is where you live? I bet it's got a great view of the water."

"Yes, and nope. Well, maybe if you get on a chair and turn your head just right." I smiled, taking another bite of my ice cream. "But my other place burned down, so I'm here temporarily while I get my head on straight."

James' eyes widened. "I'm so sorry."

I shrugged, not wanting to tell him the entire saga, like my car died too, and my fiancé ran off with my best friend a few years back.

"It's life, but I'm happy I found this place. It's hard to

get housing here in the summer."

He shook his head, biting his lip. "You've had your fair share of things recently."

I smiled. "Nope. Not recently. It's just kind of how it works for me." I pointed behind me at the flowers. "And thank you for these. Truly. It was so sweet of you, and it brightened my day."

James looked a little puzzled until he saw the flowers behind me and smiled. As I went in for another bite of ice cream, the top scoop rolled right off the cone, landing on my flip-flop. The ice cream melted instantly into a puddle of gooey pink.

"Too bad it didn't land on my bad foot." I groaned in embarrassment.

James chuckled and shook his head, trying to keep in laughter, but it came through his words. "Mind if I help?"

He didn't wait for me to answer. Instead, he moved by me and found the kitchen, which wasn't hard to find in a place this size, and grabbed the roll of paper towels and a trash bag.

Before I could protest, he'd dropped to one knee and completely cleaned my foot and the floor. He tossed the paper towels into the garbage bag and put it outside the door.

"How much do you charge for this service?" I teased.

91

"I'm a dad, so I've gotten pretty good at cleanup." He smiled at me, and I felt a familiar charge. "And I have a lot of making up to do, being Jerky James and all."

My chest tightened. "You don't owe me anything. Really. And I'm sorry my sister called you that."

He smiled. "It was earned. And I just wanted to clear one last thing up, and I'll be out of your hair."

"Okay…" I had no idea what he needed to tell me unless there'd been a mix-up on the size of the arrangement that arrived.

"I never made fun of your sister's braces."

My cheeks reddened. "So, you knew it was me who knocked you out with the apple?"

He laughed. "You didn't exactly knock me out, but your brother told me it had been you."

I smiled and shook my head, feeling all sorts of emotions running through me. It was like this weird, shared history that lasted a nanosecond, but it felt so important.

"Anyway, I wasn't making fun of your sister. She had a piece of red apple in her braces, and I was trying to point it out to her." He laughed, and his eyes connected with mine.

I clenched my eyes shut and laughed. "And then I threw a curve ball right at your forehead."

He laughed. "Yeah. Don't worry. It only left a small

lump."

"Do you know what this tells me?"

"I can only imagine."

"My brother is right. I'm a magnet for chaos."

CHAPTER EIGHT

James

As I stood at Amelia's door, watching her indulge in something as simple as eating ice cream, my heart nearly came out of its chest. The way she savored each lick of her cone, her lips glistening with a sheen of melted cherry, had a drug-like effect on me. How I stayed upright was a miracle.

And she had absolutely no idea, completely oblivious about what she did to me and probably most men in the world.

It was the same way back at the hospital.

A hospital!

How could I get turned on in an emergency room? These were questions that haunted me on my walk back to my Jeep.

In my defense, the way Amelia's tongue caressed the

pink ice cream, the aggressive way she nibbled at the edge of the cone, and the way she smiled with each swallow made me absolutely insane. I'd never paid attention to stuff like that. Who cared how someone ate a dessert?

I sat back in my office chair, groaned, and rubbed my palms over my face. "Get a hold of yourself, man. It's just a woman. You see them every single day. There's nothing special about Amelia." My voice drifted into my empty office.

I barely knew Amelia, yet our connection felt intense. In the bar, when she looked at me, I lost all sense of reality. Amelia's radiant smile transcended the boundaries of rationality, and I'd always prided myself on being rational. And even though I thought she was just trying to get something from my family, she chose to do the kind thing.

That was what enamored me the most about Amelia. She seemed kind. Apart from my grandparents and cousin's family, I hadn't been exposed to much kindness. It wasn't exactly easy to feel wanted when your mother just dumped you with her parents and hoped for the best. Or your partner in life decides she no longer wants to be a mom.

A sharp pain darted through my palm, and I realized I'd been squeezing my fist together too much.

That was usually what happened when I thought about my mom or ex.

To say I had abandonment issues was putting it lightly.

A double tap at my office door dragged me out of the rabbit hole.

I looked up to see my cousin walk into the office. He took a seat and looked at me. "You look terrible."

"I've been doing some serious soul-searching lately." I shrugged. "I guess it takes a lot of energy."

Lucas frowned. "Oh, really? You finally found one?"

I smiled and shook my head. "Unless it has to do with Henry, I'm a lost cause."

"You're a good guy whether you want to see that or not."

I shot him a wry grin. "So good that my own mother couldn't stand being around me and I scared off Henry's mom?"

"That's not how it went in either case." Lucas clutched his chest and scowled. "Come on, James. That's on her. You were a kid. She was the one with the issues, not you. Same goes for your ex."

I shrugged. "Maybe."

"This is not the James I know." Lucas stood and walked over to the cabinet where a fridge was hidden. He grabbed an iced coffee and turned to see if I wanted some. I shook my head. "What's gotten into you?"

"I don't know. Just a bad day or week or year or something."

He focused his eyes on me and took a seat. "Spill it."

"I've been contemplating my lack of a love life."

"Ah, yes. The guy who's too tired for one-night stands, too busy for dating, and too soft for relationships."

I scowled. "Too soft for relationships? What the hell does that mean?"

"You don't want to know. It's all this psychological stuff that goes back to your mother."

"Great. Why don't you enlighten me?"

He shook his head. "I don't think you're ready for this."

I motioned my fingers at him. "Lay it on me."

"The one woman whose only responsibility was to love you unconditionally put her needs in front of yours. You were heartbroken at a young age, and you've never gotten over it."

My hands steepled together, and I rested my chin on the peak of my knuckles. "Simple as that?"

He nodded. "Simple as that."

"And you came up with this, how?" I eyed him suspiciously. "Have I been a topic in your therapy sessions?"

His brows furrowed. "No. This is like basic Psych 101 stuff."

"And here I thought you were about to cheer me up and tell me how I'm charming, witty, and devastatingly handsome."

"I'm your male cousin," he said flatly.

I smiled and wiggled my brows. "Would your opinion change if you were my female cousin?"

Lucas laughed and shook his head. "It's nice to finally see a smile."

"But seriously, you think that's why I'm single? Not because I'm dedicated to my career or anything normal like that. You're telling me I have mommy issues?"

"Oh, where do I begin? Perhaps it's your profound ability to screw up most first dates. Fact. Did you know most women don't want to hear about the mating habits of penguins?" Lucas' brows rose. "For that matter, they don't want to hear about Canadian Geese and their partnership for life either. I remember when we did that double date a few years ago, I felt like I was sitting in on a National Geographic documentary. And then I'd have to remind myself that no, indeed, it was just my nerdy cousin."

I rolled my eyes. "Penguins are fascinating. And they mate for life, just like I intend to... eventually. Same with the

Canadian Geese. Henry eats this stuff up."

"Then maybe you need to start hanging out at the Audubon Society. Find a fellow birdie."

I glanced at my phone, feeling an insane itch to message Amelia.

"Whatever happened to Emily's sister?" he asked.

My eyes widened. "Oh, you're already on a first-name basis with Emily? Chatting about the family, are we?"

He shrugged and took a sip of his iced coffee. "We might go out next week, but what about Amelia?"

"Oh, the woman I put in the hospital by sending flowers?"

"You've got to be kidding me. Was she allergic?"

I smiled just thinking about her. "No. I guess she loved the bouquet and fell down the stairs admiring them."

Lucas nodded. "Nice."

"Anyway, she's got a great family. Her head is on straight. I don't need to go screwing any of that up."

"Why am I not worried about that with Emily?"

"Good question." I glanced at my monitor to check the time. "Although this encounter has been delightful, I have a meeting with a distributor I have to get to in a few minutes."

"You mean in the conference room a few doors down?" he asked wryly. "I hear the message. I'll get out of your hair. I was just stopping by to invite you to a family dinner we're having over on Marigold Island tomorrow."

"At Grandpa's place?"

"Yup."

"Sure. Sounds good."

Lucas looked like he was about to fall over. "Seriously? You always have a reason for why you don't want to go there."

"Meh." I shrugged. "What else do I have to do? Henry will enjoy it. He's been talking about the zoo your parents took him to nonstop."

And maybe I'd bump into Amelia grabbing coffee or something.

"Okay. Awesome. Your aunt will be thrilled to finally see you." He started out of my office and spun around. "Oh, and just call the girl."

I frowned. "What girl?"

"Amelia. It's written all over your face."

I chuckled and watched my cousin walk down the hallway.

Everything always seemed so easy for him. He had parents and a sister who really loved him. He had a blast at college. He was just a fun guy to be around.

I thought about his penguin comment and shook my

head. Was that actually a topic to stay away from on dates?

Without giving it a second thought, I reached for my phone and texted Amelia a simple question.

Do you like penguins?

In an instant, I got a reply.

How could I not? Did you know they are the most romantic birds on the planet? They actually mate for life. Isn't that sweet? But why do you ask? Do you need to sell one? Please tell me it's not a taxidermy penguin you need us to sell because I strongly put my foot down.

I chuckled, realizing I'd have a long way to go to impress her if she thought that I'd ask her to sell a stuffed penguin.

Thanks for the continued vote of confidence in my overall character. I do not hunt penguins, but thanks for that visual.

I tapped my finger a couple of times, wondering if that would be it, but another message flew over.

Sorry. It was just an odd question coming from a client. Sort of out of the blue. Between the flowers, riding with me in the ambulance, and cleaning up my ice cream, you've proven you're a decent guy who doesn't hunt penguins.

I smiled. Maybe I had a shot. She sent another one over.

Right?

I laughed, feeling almost giddy, and realized I had to see her again.

Are you free tomorrow for lunch?

She wrote back.

I'm still off work. I don't think it would be very nice if my sisters saw me out to lunch when I'm supposed to be hanging out at home with my foot up.

So, she's beautiful, sweet, kind, funny, and

conscientious. Great.

> *How about if I bring some food over to your place*
> *around one? I'll be on Marigold anyway.*

A minute or two passed, and it nearly killed me.

> *Sorry. Yeah. That sounds great. I accidentally texted*
> *my sister my last reply before sending it to you.*

I smiled, realizing that sounded exactly like Amelia, and I loved it.

> *See ya then.*

I slid my phone over and realized I was late for my next meeting, but I suddenly didn't care.

CHAPTER NINE

Amelia

I looked around my shoebox of an apartment and tried to fluff up the sagging blue pillows on the couch. This furniture had seen better days, but at least none of it was up in smoke like most of mine. I let out a sigh and stared between the clock on the wall and the flowers from James.

I'd spent the last couple of days inhaling as many reality tv shows as I could and felt my brain had become sufficiently numb. But not numb enough to deny that I'd seriously started crushing on James. It didn't help that he'd asked about penguins in some random text. They'd always been my favorite creature since I wrote a report on the Emperor Penguin way back in fifth grade.

My hands flew to my temples and squeezed hard.

"No, don't go there, Amelia," I commanded as if I'd actually listen to something I'd tell myself. "This isn't a sign. He's not a sign. The penguins aren't a sign. He's a grumpy guy with red flags waving in every direction to get my attention."

A loud knock thudded through the apartment, and my pulse started pounding between my temples. I reached for the crutches my mom dropped off last night and shook my head. The guy probably just felt guilty because he sent the flowers that sent me to the hospital.

I hobbled through the living room with only the tapping of the crutches to match my racing heart as I got to the door. But I didn't open it. I just stared at the wood separating James and me, willing myself to play it cool. But I couldn't help but feel a mix of excitement and nervousness.

Closing my eyes, I took a deep breath and reached for the doorknob. The moment I pulled it open, my eyes blinked open to see James.

And my gawd. He looked sensational. Too good to be true. Plus, he was holding a bag of food from one of my favorite places on the island, a cute little sandwich shop down the way.

But the red flag three hundred and eighty-nine waved in front of me. No man should look this amazing in a pair of jeans and a tee, and the aviators weren't helping. He lifted his sunglasses up and propped them on his forehead somehow. If I tried that, they'd fall off and tumble to the ground.

"Did you plan on inviting me in, or should I just hand over the food and run?"

I blushed, feeling my cheeks turn a shade of crimson. "Right. Come on in. You just threw me for a loop."

"Did I?" The way his gaze lingered on mine did all sorts of crazy things to me. I wanted to suddenly toss the sandwiches on the counter and wrap my arms around his neck for a kiss.

The lunch wasn't off to a smooth start if this was where my mind wanted to venture. What was wrong with me?

James smiled as his blue eyes filled with genuine warmth. "How's the foot holding up?"

I chuckled, trying to make light of my situation. "Well, it's certainly keeping me on my toes, err, I mean, foot. No, it's actually keeping me off my foot." I shook my head, wondering why I couldn't put two thoughts together around him. I averted my eyes from his and immediately felt calmer. "I managed to spill my dinner all over the counter last night, and then my crutch caught the garbage can this morning and dumped it on the kitchen floor. " I grinned, bringing my eyes back to his. "But I don't know if I can blame that on the crutches or just being me. But, my foot is actually much better."

James let out a genuine laugh, his eyes crinkling at the corners. I noticed his hair had even more chocolate highlights than before, or maybe it was my imagination.

"How about you get comfortable on the couch, and I'll bring over our meal? I don't need to have Doctor Stan wondering why you keep injuring yourself because of me."

I chuckled. "Truthfully, I doubt he'd even think twice."

James smiled as he placed the bag on the kitchen counter and looked over at me as I was getting myself comfortable on the couch. There was something really sweet about being around him, which made absolutely no sense, considering the first interactions we'd had together were anything but.

As I propped my ankle on a pillow, I winced at the pain.

"That doesn't look like it's feeling better." He walked over with two plates of food and glanced at my foot.

"It really is," I promised.

"Is there anything I can do to help? I feel so bad this is happening because of me."

I shook my head, holding the plate he'd handed me. "This wasn't because of you. I was born this way. Bonafide klutz. If it wasn't the arrangement, it would have been something else that caused me to tumble down the stairs."

He laughed and shook his head. "If you say so."

An electrical current ran through me when he sat down next to me and his leg brushed against mine. I pretended I didn't notice that he was studying me as I unwrapped my sandwich. It had been so long since I'd felt noticed that I really kind of liked it.

"Did you ask my brother what my favorite lunch place was?"

He smiled and shook his head. "No. Why?"

"Because this is it." I grinned happily. "Never mind that it's owned by my ex-fiancé's parents. They can't help that's he's a creepy son."

James laughed as my eyes widened. I'd never meant for that revelation to escape my lips. "So, he's not a current fiancé?" His eyes appeared to have brightened.

"Nope. Not as of three years ago when he and my best friend decided it was their destiny to break my heart into a million little pieces and scatter each one along the ferry ride back to Seattle."

"Ouch."

I chuckled. "Sorry. Too much information." I rolled my eyes and took a bite of the sandwich.

Heaven.

Tomato and pesto with mozzarella.

"You really don't have the best of luck, do you?" He shook his head, looking bewildered.

"Well, I like to think of each of these incidences as great learning experiences." I took another bite. "And at some point, I'm going to be so wise that I will see these things coming miles away."

He laughed. "I like the way you view life."

"Well, it's called survival."

James nodded quietly and took a bite of his sandwich. "This is really good."

"My favorite," I chirped in between bites.

"I can see why."

"Did you have a chance to look at the letters?" I asked.

He sucked in a sudden breath and glanced out the window that looked at pretty much nothing unless, of course, you did my acrobatic trick to see the water.

"No. I haven't had a chance yet."

I saw a glint of disappointment or maybe agitation flicker through his gaze. I knew I should leave it alone, but I couldn't help myself.

"Oh. Wow. I would have thought you'd want to see

them."

He nodded and brought his gaze back to mine. "We weren't close."

"Oh, I'm sorry." I didn't really know what to say. I'd viewed the letters as treasures begging to be read by the recipient, not something to be despised. "I…Does that mean you might not want the diary that's stuck in a vase?"

James' gaze flashed to mine. "There's a diary?"

"I can't be sure, but it's the size of one and kind of looks like it to me." I drew a breath, feeling my chest tighten and my heart rate speed up a bit. "But I don't know for certain."

He placed his plate on a small table and sat back on the couch. "You said you read that first letter?"

I nodded, feeling a lump in my throat. "I did."

"What was the tone?"

His question surprised me. He didn't ask what was in the letter but rather the feel of it.

My eyes flicked to his. "Honestly, the tone was endearing, sweet, and there was a longing in the words."

James shook his head. "I wish all families were like yours, Amelia." He let out a deep breath and pushed his legs out in front of him. "But they're not."

I nodded. "I recognize that. For what it's worth, it

seemed like she loved you a lot."

He shoved his fingers through his hair and brought his legs back in. "Actions speak louder than words. Love is being there for your son like I'm there for mine."

"I suppose that's very true." The pit in my stomach was growing tighter and wider as if it might swallow me up, and before I knew what was spewing out of my mouth, it happened.

"She said she loved you very much and was so proud of your spelling and baseball skills." I stared at him like he had three heads. I just couldn't imagine someone thinking their mother didn't love them.

A little curl of his lip formed on the right, which turned into a solid smirk. "Ah, she must have gotten nostalgic right before she dumped me off at the boarding school."

"You went to a boarding school?" I'd only heard of kids being shipped off to them, but I'd never actually met a product of one.

"Until I graduated high school." He shook his head, and a glint of darkness replaced his gaze. "And did you know how many times she visited or had me visit her with her new husband once she sent me off?"

"I'm not sure I want to know the answer," I said softly, realizing there was far more to this relationship than some sweet words once scribbled onto a piece of paper.

"Never. If it weren't for my grandparents, I would have been one of the kids who just stayed back at the school on all holidays and breaks." He shrugged. "But I'm enormously grateful to them. I had a good life. I won't pretend I didn't. I grew up in opportunity, and I fully recognize that. I want to provide that same opportunity for Henry, but I also want to be there for him."

The way his words softened on his son made my stomach swirl into admiration. A guy who loved his son this much couldn't be all grump.

Besides, his version of growing up sounded like anything but a life full of privilege. Love built opportunities that lasted and created foundations for lives that were full of freedom. I knew my parents loved me and my siblings more than anything. It was their love that gave me the freedom to fail because I always knew they'd be there.

My eyes met his. "I couldn't imagine not having someone to fall back on when times were tough." Shaking my head, I reached out to his hand and curled my fingers around his. "And I couldn't imagine anything tougher than having your own mother abandon you."

A smile broke through James' expression, and he kept our hands touching. "Well, this lunch took a sudden turn."

I chuckled. "It was totally me. I shouldn't have brought up my failed engagement to a potential crush."

"Potential crush?" His smile widened.

I let out a happy sigh. For some reason, I liked being around James. Whether he was snapping at me on the phone, riding with me in an ambulance, or bringing me lunch, it was really nice to be with him. I wasn't really worried about what came out of my mouth.

"So, I didn't completely ruin my chances by hanging up on you and not returning your calls."

I smiled, feeling my stomach flutter at his words. Ruin his chances? He wants a chance. I felt like the coolest uncool chick around.

"Everyone has a bad day." I pressed my lips together and looked at my foot. "And some of us just have more than others."

CHAPTER TEN

James

"Something tells me this is completely unhealthy." I glanced at my cousin, who took a shot of vodka.

"Mom is after me again about why I'm not settling down," he said, rolling his eyes. "Remind me why I think these dinners are a good idea."

I shrugged and laughed. "Beats me, but you invited me to this one, and besides, Henry has been having a blast all day with your parents."

The orchard was the perfect place to spend time at his age. Every tree looked gigantic and held so much possibility. Even though I managed to stop by to see Amelia, I'd spent most of the day with Henry, and it was perfection. He was perfection.

Right now, he was being spoiled by Lucas' sister, my other cousin Nina.

"James, have you noticed how our family keeps pushing us to get married?" Lucas said, his forehead creased with worry.

I chuckled and adjusted my sunglasses. "Oh, trust me, I've noticed, but it's more on you. They've laid off since Henry. There's a lot of perks to having my little guy." I glanced at him as his giggles rang into the air from Nina's tickles.

Lucas groaned. "But why? Can't they see we're perfectly content with our single lives?"

I scratched my head as Lucas grabbed a soda to wash down his shot. "Are we, though?"

My aunt waved from the patio out back, which I knew meant it was time to head that way for dinner.

My grandparents' estate was very much like they'd left it. The rooms were all grand, the furniture exquisite and over the top, and everything perfectly in place. It was very much how it was when I lived here in between my romps at the boarding school.

"Dude, I'm totally good on my own." He patted my left shoulder, but I wasn't sure he completely believed his own words.

I leaned back against a column, pretending to ponder his question as his mom spoke with Lucas' sister and wrangled Henry.

"Well, maybe they think we're incomplete without a partner. Or maybe they just want more weddings to attend. Who knows?"

Lucas rubbed his temples. "But James, I'm not ready for marriage or any of the responsibilities that come with it. I can barely take care of my houseplants."

"You have houseplants?" I smirked.

"Of course I do."

"Come on, Lucas, it's not that hard. You just have to remember to water your partner every now and then and pluck off the dead leaves."

"Water my girlfriend? I thought we were having a deep discussion."

"When has having a deep conversation after two beers and a shot been a good idea?"

He laughed and nodded. "Point taken."

Lucas shook his head, his eyes wide. "Besides, with my luck, I'd probably get stuck with a cactus for a wife, all prickly and sharp and just waiting to poke me."

"Geez. No wonder you don't want to be in a relationship. Way to set the bar high, buddy." I laughed, pushing myself off the column. "Come on. Aunt Beth is getting all antsy. We don't want to stress your mom out."

I walked over to Henry, interrupting a massive squeal as I lifted him up and carried him toward the large opening that led to the lush patio. The truth was that it cost a fortune to keep this place up, but it was nice to have a spot the family could gather, even if I rarely joined them.

And maybe now that Henry was older, I'd make more of a habit of coming over.

"It would be so nice if one day, you had a girlfriend to even out the dinner table discussions," Aunt Beth teased her son.

Henry grinned. "Uncle Luke is silly."

Aunt Beth handed me a glass of wine. "Thanks."

"How's my favorite nephew?" she asked as I slid Henry into a chair next to mine.

"It makes it easy since I'm your only nephew, but I'm doing good."

"Henry said you had a girlfriend."

My eyes widened. "What?"

She nodded. "And then your cousin said that's who you dropped off some lunch for earlier."

I laughed and shook my head.

"No such luck," I answered, but my mind

immediately drifted to Amelia. "No girlfriend."

She laughed and turned away, but she was still within earshot distance, so I turned to my cousin and grinned. "So, how is everything going with Emily? Have you gone out?"

Aunt Beth spun around with the wine bottle still in her hand. "Emily? Who's Emily?"

Lucas glared at me, but a smile crept onto his lips. "You're one wicked man."

"I had to save myself," I whispered with a laugh.

"There is no Emily, Mom."

Aunt Beth set the bottle down in the middle of the table as Nina sat by her mom with her eyes fastened on her brother.

"Emily?" Her brows perked up. "Are you finally dating someone?"

"No." Lucas sat next to me even though he probably wanted to murder me.

Both women looked at me as my uncle brought over a platter of salmon from the grill.

"Where did you get the name Emily?" Nina asked. "Obviously, James didn't make up the name. Right, James?"

I shook my head. "Nope. I did not. There is very much an Emily."

Lucas laughed and shook his head, reaching for some

salmon. "Oh, it's on."

I chuckled and put some asparagus on Henry's plate and mine.

"Emily is Amelia's sister, and Amelia is the woman James was visiting."

My eyes shot to Lucas. Well played.

Aunt Beth pursed her lips. "Oh, Amelia. What a lovely name."

I nodded. "She's a lovely person."

Nina narrowed her eyes on me. "Is it the same Amelia who works at the antique store on the island?"

Damn.

"Yeah, it is." I nodded. "We're just acquaintances."

Lucas shook his head. "Not true at all. He even rode in the ambulance when she fell down the stairs."

Now it was my turn to glare at my cousin.

"And she fell down the stairs because she was admiring some flowers he'd sent her."

I took a bite of salmon and laughed, shaking my head. "I bought the flowers as an apology."

"Did you get in a fight?" Aunt Beth asked. "So soon?"

Lucas was good at what he did. "No. He hung up on her and wouldn't take her calls. It's a long story."

"Sounds juicy." Aunt Beth's eyes widened.

Nina chuckled. "And she's still willing to talk to you?"

"Yes."

"Why would you ever hang up on someone? That's incredibly rude."

I nodded in agreement. "It is, but I thought she was a spam call or something."

Nina shook her head, and Aunt Beth took a bite of salmon.

"But Amelia's sister named me Jerky James, and apparently, that sold Lucas on Emily."

Nina pointed her fork at me, connecting the dots. "I seriously can't believe you two are dating sisters."

Lucas scowled. "We're not dating anyone."

"Flowers are being sent. Lunches are being had. And you're telling me you two aren't dating or in relationships?" Aunt Beth shook her head in disapproval while my uncle laughed. "No wonder you two are single."

"In all fairness, I haven't been on a date with Emily." Lucas took a bite of salmon.

"Why's that?"

"She won't return my calls."

"Oh, that can't be good for the ego." Nina chuckled.

"Not good at all."

"Why?" Henry asked, looking over at me. I scooped some more pasta salad onto his plate.

"Your uncle is silly. That's why."

Henry nodded and ate a noodle.

"Well, since we're back to square one on this dating topic, I thought we could chat about why I really wanted all of you here," Uncle Joe said. He was usually a man of few words. He just enjoyed watching how everything played out rather than dipping a toe in the pond.

Aunt Beth straightened and dabbed her mouth with a napkin.

"I've been in touch with the Chamber here on the island. For years, they've mentioned how much it had meant to the community when the apple orchard was open in the late summer and fall."

My brows pulled together. "Okay."

That was an event my grandparents always put on, but since they'd passed away, we never continued the tradition.

"And I think it's about time we open up the orchards again to the community and get the festival back on." My uncle glanced at his son and then over at me. "Henry is at an age where I think he'd love it. Our kids loved coming here on the weekends."

I hid a smile, thinking back to Amelia whopping me

in the head with an apple.

"But most of the work would fall on you three since we're headed to Portugal for the summer," Aunt Beth added.

I laughed. "Always a catch."

"It brings so much happiness to the community and brings people over to the island, which in turn helps local businesses, and the orchards have been maintained. They're just sitting here unused." Aunt Beth smiled. "Plus, it's good PR for our brands."

"Well, as long as we have our priorities straight." I smiled and glanced at Lucas, who looked like he was ready to fall over from one too many libations. "I'm in."

Nina nodded in agreement. "Me too. I can handle all the press and marketing."

"Great. Then it's settled. You three get together and figure out how to pull this off. We ought to make use of this great property for more than just family barbecues."

I'd done my best to stay away from this property for years, but suddenly, I didn't want to ignore my childhood home.

Well, no. That wasn't true. My childhood home from birth until my mother abandoned me was quite a different story. That place I never wanted to step foot in again, and it was why I called up a company to auction off its contents. I probably would have gotten more money had I told them who she actually was—an heiress to my family's fortune. Instead, I used her married name, and the company never did any digging, but it was all over and done with, and that's all I wanted. The thought of that place pained me and drained me.

But the idea of reviving this old place kind of excited me.

Or maybe it was the thought of seeing Amelia again. This seemed like a project she'd be excited about.

"A party?" Henry asked, chasing half of a cherry tomato on his plate.

"Yeah." I nodded. "A party. When I was your age, this place would be one big party on the weekends for everyone who lived here. There'd be apple cider making, corn mazes, orchard races, and a petting zoo."

Henry's eyes widened. "Wow."

"Well, good. Now that that's solved, I think I'll take my wine to the orchard. Joe, care to join me?"

Nina hopped up. "I would."

"Good. We'll let the guys take care of the dishes tonight. There's more of you, and it seems we'll be outnumbered for a while."

I smiled, glancing at Lucas, who didn't look like he'd be taking care of much of anything, so Henry and I wandered into the kitchen as Lucas attempted to bring the dishes inside while I rinsed off the plates.

"Payback is gonna get ya," Lucas teased, dropping off the last bowl.

"Probably not until after you sleep this off," I joked. "I'm guessing you had more than I knew about before I got here?"

He nodded with a groan and rested his arm over his head. "Nina tricked me. She played me. We did a shot contest."

"I think it's safe to say hers was water."

Lucas groaned.

"We're not in our twenties anymore," I teased, knowing Lucas didn't need to be reminded of that. But there had always been a very strange and real sibling rivalry between Nina and Lucas. Generally, Nina came out on top.

As I handed a couple of plastic spoons to Henry, he attempted to wipe them off with the towel before taking them to the couch to play drums next to Lucas, which made me love my son even more.

I wandered back outside and collected what Lucas left behind, but all I could think about was Amelia and when I could see her again.

CHAPTER ELEVEN

Amelia

My ankle was as good as new, and I was back at the antique store, admiring a few new items. There was a beautiful fruit bowl that I imagined on my dining table I didn't have any longer in an apartment that I wasn't in yet.

"Don't do too much, kiddo," my dad called from behind a rack of shawls.

I'd probably be fifty, and my dad would still call me that, but it was what I loved about him. We were all his little girls.

Brad was still Tiger now and again, so we all had our plight.

"I know, Dad. I'm just dusting."

I hobbled through the rows of vintage treasures in our

beloved antique store, feeling a sense of nostalgia wash over me. I spent all my time here when I was a little girl. While other kids played with their friends, I always wanted to be here. It turned out to be the same when I grew up.

The store had always been a special place for my parents and me, filled with memories and stories of the past. Today, however, there was something different in the air, a bittersweet longing emanating from my dad. I couldn't imagine it was just because I fell down the stairs. It wasn't my first clumsy rodeo.

I found him near a collection of antique bird illustrations.

"Dad," I said softly, placing a hand on his shoulder. "I'm totally fine. Really. I promise."

"I know you are."

"But are you okay?"

He turned to me with fondness in his eyes. "Amelia, my dear, I was just reminiscing about your mother. Sometimes, it feels like yesterday, and other times, it feels like a lifetime ago, but we've had so much time together." He sighed. "But it's not nearly enough."

"But you guys have so much more living to do."

He nodded as a smile tugged at the corner of his lips. "No, I know. We do. If we're lucky enough, we do."

"Dad, is this because your birthday is coming up?"

My dad laughed and nodded. "Probably. Thank goodness they keep coming, but it gets me a little sentimental too."

"It doesn't help that you chose a profession like this either, basking in old treasures and other people's memories."

He chuckled and nodded. "I think the profession found me, or maybe it was your mother who orchestrated it all. I can never be sure with her."

I laughed. "She's a sneaky one."

He smiled and rubbed my back. "I hope you find a love like ours, Amelia. I really do. I hope that for all my girls."

The sudden change in topic took me off-guard.

I winked, playing it off. "If it's meant to be, it will be."

He shrugged, taking his hand off my back to rearrange a little Swarovski figurine. "Yes and no."

I scowled. "What's that supposed to mean?"

"You have to be open to it."

"To what?"

"Love."

"Dad." I glanced around the antique store as if someone was listening, but no one was. "I'm open."

"You're not." He shook his head. "And with good

reason. You had a deep betrayal. You were hurt. You're still hurt."

I took a deep breath, feeling the weight of his words. I liked to pretend that I'd gotten over all of it. I mean, who needed a best friend, anyway? And a fiancé? A dime a dozen. But his words sank deep into my heart.

He knew.

"Do you think I'll ever find a love like yours, Dad? A love that's so deep and profound? And just… right?"

He paused for a moment, his eyes searching mine. "My love, I believe with all my heart that you will find someone who will see your tenderness as a strength and not something to be trampled upon. They'll understand your heart is bigger than you. Amelia, you have so much to offer, and the right person will recognize and cherish that. But you have to believe that too."

I sighed, feeling a mix of hope and doubt swirling within me. "How will I know, Dad? How will I know when it's real and lasting? I thought my fiancé was The One, my forever."

He placed his hand over mine, a gentle reassurance. "Did you, though?"

His words stabbed me in the heart. Not because of the question but because of my answer. My dad knew that man was never the one, and I did, too, on some level.

"Love, my dear Amelia, is a journey filled with ambiguity and uncertainty. But you must trust your instincts, your intuition." He grabbed my hand. "Does this place feel like home?"

I nodded, glancing around the shelves and shelves of countless antiques. "Yes. I knew I needed to come back here. My soul told me as much."

"Well, that is love. When you find the right person, it will feel like coming home. They will make you laugh, support you in your dreams, and love you unconditionally whether you fall down the stairs or set a pot on fire." He winked at me. "But the first step is recognizing the interest exists. The second step is not pushing it away."

"Or making excuses," I mumbled to myself.

"Exactly." He sighed and saw a customer walking toward the counter with two large, embroidered pillows. "Now, off to my destiny."

I chuckled and watched my dad wander to the checkout counter.

My eye caught a new piece I hadn't seen before, but my mind drifted to James.

Ever since he'd dropped off lunch and we shared a few laughs, I couldn't get him out of my head. I'd see a commercial and think of him. I'd hear a guy laugh in the store and think of James. It was ridiculous. Plus, it didn't help that the flower arrangement was gigantic and beautiful and still sitting in my apartment to remind me of the guy who gave it to me.

And everything and nothing he managed to reveal at the same time about his childhood, and even Henry's, etched a curiosity in me that I never expected. It was like the first night I met him, there was a darkness, a pain running through his gaze.

That was the problem, though. I had a very active imagination. Rather than just saying to myself, he'll be a good guy for someone, I'd start to imagine all sorts of scenarios. Like, should I try to coerce him into wanting the diary over dinner and drinks? Would he pick up the phone if I called him to go out sometime, or would he hang up on me again? Did he actually feel guilty about everything, and that was why he was being so kind, or was there something else there?

And what about Henry? He needed stability.

And my mind would spin into a complicated cocoon of emotion and fantasy.

Because I felt *something*. When his hand touched mine, electricity pulsed through me. When our eyes stayed on one another for a beat too long, I'd feel flushed and get butterflies. And his smiles... Oh, my goodness. When he smiled, it felt like I had a mini-volcanic eruption in my belly where lava flowed to my chest and to my knees.

So, this! This was why I didn't want my mind wandering to James. I wasn't sane about it at all. There was nothing there between us, apart from a few chance meetings and a lunch. I didn't need to start imagining there was more just because butterflies started bumping into each other like spastic insects.

And he had a son. I didn't want to interfere or cause complications. Family was the most important thing above lust.

I slid my hand off an embroidered peacock and sighed.

"Amelia," my brother's voice barked at me, and I nearly dropped the peacock.

"Geez. What was that about?" I laughed, feeling my heart race.

"I've been calling your name for the last minute, and you were in la-la land."

I rolled my eyes and glanced at what he was holding.

"I managed to pull this out of the vase without damaging it or chipping the ceramic." He dangled it over me. "You can thank me later and buy me a beer over at Milo's."

I snatched it away and laughed. "Thanks. The customer said he doesn't really have an interest in it, but I'll keep it just in case."

Brad smiled. "Customer? As in James, the man who rode with you in the ambulance, bought you flowers, and came over with lunch? That customer?"

I rolled my eyes and clutched the tiny diary. "Well, I haven't heard from him since lunch, so in my usual spirit, I'm sure I scared him away."

A wry grin spread across Brad's face. "I don't think that's the case."

My brows shot up. "Oh, yeah? Why do you say that?"

"Just a guy hunch."

"Or wishful thinking to get me out of your hair."

My brother laughed and shook his head. "You're the easy sister."

I touched my heart with my free hand and grinned. "You're always so sweet when you want something, so spill it."

"I'm offended."

"You fished the diary out of a priceless vase for me, and you told me I was an easy sister." I shook my head. "You gave yourself away with a completed task and a compliment in one sitting."

"Fine. I'm headed out with the guys on a road trip."

I shrugged. "Okay. That's fine with me."

"Will you cover my weekend shift and take Oscar?"

I hissed in a breath of hot air. "Oscar?"

Brad's eyes pleaded with me as I stared back at him in disbelief. Everyone knew to say no to babysitting Oscar.

"That cat hates me. That cat hates the entire family." I shuddered. "Actually, I think he hates the entire human race."

"Would you blame him?"

I scowled. "What are you blabbing about? You're the most extroverted person I know. You love people."

He ignored me.

"Will you do it?" He wiggled his brows and lifted his shoulders. "You can have the run of my house. You can stay there all weekend. Spread out more than where you're at now."

I let out a low sigh as I debated about whether I really wanted another go at the emergency room because of a sinister cat. Oscar had a way with his claws, and his teeth were never far behind. Poor Dottie had to be taken to the emergency vet when Oscar snuck up on her while she was sleeping.

Sleeping!!

That was who Oscar was at his core. He couldn't be

133

trusted.

"Fine. It's not like I have anything better to do." I glanced at the door. "Where are you going with the boys?"

"Montana."

"Isn't that a bit of a drive?"

"Nah. We'll just start early. We'll be in the car nine hours, tops."

I laughed, knowing how their guys' trips always went. I didn't even ask my brother what he planned on doing once he got there because I wasn't sure I wanted to know.

"Hey, Amelia. A client is here to see you." My dad craned his neck around the shelf and arched his brows.

My brows knitted together. "A client? I don't have clients."

Brad clapped his hands and rubbed them together as he stuck his head out and looked toward the counter where my dad had been. "Oh, this is good. Have fun with your *client*, Amelia, and thanks for watching Oscar."

"Thanks for getting this out of the vase." I waved the small journal or whatever it was and put it in the back pocket of my jeans.

"I have a few things to take care of upstairs," my dad muttered as I started toward the counter.

"Okay. You know where to find me."

As I made my way from behind the shelf, I heard a snicker from my brother as my eyes connected with James.

Client.

He looked incredible with his lopsided smile and navy tee hanging over his worn jeans. I had to rip my gaze away from James' body to meet his eyes and pretend that I saw his type every single day.

"What are you up to?" I asked, feeling my breath hitch in the back of my throat, so I cleared it too loudly and made it sound like a hack.

"Just in the neighborhood, and I thought I'd stop by."

My lip curled slightly. "In the neighborhood? This island isn't exactly in the neighborhood of much. Possibly because you'd have to be a really good swimmer to get here or know the ferry schedule by heart, but it's not exactly convenient."

He leaned against the counter and smiled at me. "Fine. I'll come clean. I wanted to see you again."

I stared at him.

"And I'm actually going to be on this island a lot more in the coming months."

"Why's that?" I swallowed my surprise.

"We're opening the orchard up to the community again this fall." His eyes stayed on mine, and I felt a current run through us. It was like the rest of the world had just drifted away.

"Oh, yeah?"

He nodded. "The Fall Festival will be bigger and better than ever."

I smiled, nodding, but for some reason, it felt like he had put me in a trance. "I believe it. What made you decide to open the property again?"

"My aunt and uncle thought it would be a good idea, and seeing how much Henry loves being there made me realize they were right. The community should get to enjoy the orchard too."

I loved how his gaze softened when he spoke of his son.

"That's so sweet of your family. I remember growing up and looking forward to the weekend festivals every year."

"Well, my cousins and I are in charge of getting the word out and the place ready for crowds again."

"Nice."

"And I have to confess that the thought of getting to see you this summer excites me."

I laughed and folded my arms over my chest. "Who said you get to see me more?"

The low hum of his laughter lit me up, warming my

belly and putting me squarely in a place I shouldn't want to be in.

"Can't hate a guy for trying."

I scowled. "What makes you think you want to see me again?"

James scratched the dark scruff along his chin and laughed. "I don't know. Maybe it's because there's something about you that makes me want to know more."

"Is that so?" I put my hands on my hips. "There's not much there to learn. I'm an open book. Go ahead, ask me anything."

"What's your favorite restaurant here on the island?"

"That's easy. Cardelli's on the Waterfront."

He smiled. "That was my grandparents' favorite too. So, it's a date. I'll pick you up on Saturday night."

A couple of customers wandered up to the counter, and I straightened and glanced at them with a smile.

"That was a trick question," I whispered.

"Is it a date?"

I pressed my lips together as I walked behind the counter to the register and looked over at him. "Yeah. It's a date. But I won't be at my place. I'm staying at my brother's this weekend to housesit his cranky cat."

"Good times." James laughed.

"Pretty much how my weekends go around here," I called after him.

He turned around and flashed me another grin. "Text me the address, and I'll pick you up at seven."

Feeling like I was floating into another galaxy, I turned my attention to the older woman standing in front of me with a giant ceramic frog. Her white hair was swept into a tidy bun with a few wispy strands hanging down.

"He's a keeper, that one. Real easy on the eyes, if you know what I mean." She raised her white eyebrows, and I chuckled.

"Time will tell."

She slid the frog onto the counter, and I glanced out the window to see James climbing into his Jeep.

"Don't fight it, girl. Take it from me. I've been married seven times, and this last one is a keeper. Find yourself a keeper the first time around."

I chuckled, scanning the frog. "I'll keep that in mind."

"And show a little cleavage. Men always like that."

I laughed, wrapping her frog into some tissue. "If only it were that easy."

CHAPTER TWELVE

James

The stuffed penguin sat in the passenger seat as I pulled down the driveway to pick up Amelia. The days had flown by, especially because I'd volunteered to help the preschool group visit the Aquarium yesterday. Henry loved every second of it, especially when he got to pet the starfish.

I shook my head as I pulled in front of the garage and turned off the Jeep. It had been so many years since I went on an actual date. What was I thinking? This was probably a really bad idea. I didn't need to be bringing random women into Henry's life. He needed stability.

Although Nina was more than happy to babysit him tonight at my place. She showed up with three kinds of pizza for a three-year-old and became his instant hero.

The thought brought a smile to my lips.

Man, I loved that boy.

I'd do anything for him.

And maybe what that should be was to remain celibate until he graduated college.

I reached for my cell and texted Lucas.

I think I made a mistake. This is all too soon.

Lucas instantly replied back.

You haven't been on a date in four years. There is nothing too soon about any of this. Now, quit being a pansy and enjoy yourself. Peace out.

I jumped out of the Jeep and walked up to the front door, where I heard a woman screaming. My pulse quickened, and I quickly knocked on the door.

"Amelia, it's me. Are you okay? Is everything okay?" I tried opening the door, and another shriek rang out.

I glanced at the open window next to the door and shook my head. Someone must have gotten in through there.

Without a second thought, I ducked my head into the opening and pushed the curtains aside as I crawled through, getting my foot caught behind me. I tripped to the floor as another scream erupted down the hallway, followed by the sound of tumbling pots and pans.

"Amelia," I shouted, getting to my feet and making my way toward the noise.

"I'm in here," she called back.

I shook off part of the curtain still stuck to my foot and darted down the hall to what was the kitchen.

Amelia stood on the counter with a skillet in each hand and paper towels wrapped around her knuckles. She stared at the kitchen table, but I didn't see a soul.

"What's going on? Have you called the police?" My pulse pounded so hard I could feel the blood rushing between my ears a mile a second.

"There's nothing they can do." She breathed heavily and glanced over at me with fear in her gaze. "This cat is from another realm."

My body instantly relaxed at her words, and I started laughing.

She narrowed her eyes on me. "You think it's funny now? Just wait."

"What's its name?"

"Demon Cat of the Dark Realm," she said flatly with the skillets still up in the air.

"Seriously?"

"No. Fine." She sighed. "His name is Oscar."

"As in Oscar the Grouch?"

"You got it."

I bent over and immediately spotted the angry feline. Oscar hissed and lunged at me. With no seconds to spare, I rolled on the floor to avoid its claws.

But when I stopped moving, Oscar jumped on my chest and opened his mouth to reveal a very small set of glistening white teeth.

"He's about to bite. Let me scare him away." Amelia clanged the skillets together as I attempted to pull Oscar from my shirt, but he dug in deeper.

"He's gonna get ya," Amelia warned. "I know that look in his eyes."

The grey furball stared directly at me, inches from my face, hissing as if to dare me to make the wrong move. Amelia stopped banging the skillets together and slid off the counter.

"It's okay, Oscar. You're okay." I moved my fingers along Oscar's forehead, which made the cat's scowl deepen.

And when I least expected it, he chomped my thumb and wouldn't let go.

"Dang it," I muttered, whipping my hand around.

Oscar smiled at me and jumped off my chest as

Amelia rushed over.

"Oh, no. It's bleeding." She shook her head, kneeling next to me.

"Why do you have paper towels on your hands?" I asked, standing up from the floor, unable to spot Oscar anywhere.

"He got me good on both knuckles, but it all happened so fast that all I could do was climb onto the counter and grab some towels to wrap around them before he started leaping toward me again."

I grimaced at the thought and walked over to the sink to wash out the wound with soap.

"I'll go grab some alcohol," Amelia called over her shoulder.

"As much as I'd like a drink right about now, I'll wait until the restaurant."

She laughed and shook her head. "No, for the wound."

As Amelia spun around, I noticed two long scratches along the back of her legs.

"Did you know he got you on your legs too?"

She groaned. "Yeah. When I was climbing onto the counter, he couldn't help himself."

"And this is your brother's cat?"

"Sure is." She handed me a squirt bottle of rubbing alcohol. "Let me see it."

"It's fine."

"Cat bites can turn nasty really quick. We should take you in."

"I'm totally fine, and besides, I'm not going to miss out on dinner with you over a silly cat with a complex." I laughed and shook my head. "Besides, it's not every Saturday night that I can find a babysitter for Henry."

She twisted her lips into a sexy little pout. "Who's watching him? Is it Lucas?"

"No, Lucas' sister. Nina's super amazing with him, and I never go out. So, she never has a reason to watch him."

"You never go out?" She looked surprised and stood a little closer as I squirted more of the alcohol onto my thumb. The sting etched deep into the wound.

"Not really. Henry and I have a groove. Friday nights include a movie and homemade pizza on the couch. Saturday night is takeout and finger painting. My weekends are essentially booked."

She smiled and nodded. "You're a good dad."

I shrugged. "I don't know about that. I just try my hardest and hope it's enough."

"No. I can tell you're one of the good ones."

I liked hearing that from her. Her words felt genuine, and my parenting was something I prided myself on.

Amelia cocked her head slightly and drew a deep breath. "Can I ask what happened between you and his mom?"

I blew out a gust of warm air that turned into an unexpected groan. "I'm still trying to figure that out, to be honest."

"Really?" She touched my arm and reached for a Band-Aid to stick over the wound.

"It's complicated, but I have full custody."

The thought of my ex made my stomach turn. It was like I'd somehow found my mother disguised in someone my age and found the one person who didn't want their own child. But I didn't need to bring all that up. Just for one night, I'd like to forget it all.

Amelia nodded thoughtfully, and her gaze connected with mine. "She's missing out on an amazing family. I hope she knows that."

Her words smacked me unexpectedly, and I smiled. "Thanks."

A screech sounded down the hall, and I laughed. "Oscar has impeccable timing."

She rolled her eyes. "You have no idea. It sounds like he's in the bathroom."

As we turned around, Oscar raced out of the powder room with a piece of toilet paper attached to his tail, which made him absolutely maniacal. He howled at the top of his lungs as he zipped down the hallway toward us.

"Not again," Amelia muttered, skittering back up the cabinet.

"Here, Oscar. Let me help you," I said softly, bending over.

"Do you have a death wish?" She laughed as I put my hand out to try to get the toilet paper off his tail.

He veered away from me and circled around as I pinched the end of the toilet paper, but it tightened the wad around his tail, and Oscar yowled again.

I let go of the toilet paper, but it was too late.

Oscar sprang into the air and bit my ass. His pointy teeth dug past the fabric of my jeans and sank into my flesh.

"I'll get 'em off," Amelia yelled, sliding off the counter.

"No. No. It's fine." I shook my head, waving my hand. There was no way Oscar was letting go.

"What do you plan on doing?" Her eyes widened. "Just let him dangle there?"

I reached around and felt the silky furball swinging from my rear when Amelia started to laugh. My fingers found the stray toilet paper which I unwrapped carefully and handed to Amelia.

"I'm sorry. I can't help it. I always laugh when I'm not supposed to." Her eyes brightened as she covered her mouth. "This is just my luck. I finally meet an amazing guy, and he gets attacked by my brother's cat."

My eyes met hers. "Amazing, huh?"

Oscar's teeth traded for his claws, and I took a deep breath as the clutch of his tiny jaw shifted and let go before jumping away.

"Yeah. I'd say so far, you seem pretty great." She smiled.

"You've forgiven me for hanging up on you?"

"Possibly." Her eyes went down to the back of my jeans. "Oh, no. You're bleeding."

I laughed, shaking my head. "Of course I am."

She held up the alcohol bottle and grinned. "Hate to tell ya this, but we've got to clean that wound out."

The look in her eyes made me chuckle. "We, huh?"

"How do you expect to reach around there?" Her eyes stayed on mine. "Did you want me to call Lucas?"

I grinned and shook my head. "Definitely not."

"Okay, then. It's decided. Drop the pants and bend over."

"Why do I feel like you're loving every second of this?"

She reached for some paper towels and wet them before putting soap on them. "Because for once, it's not me being rushed to the emergency room."

"That's the only reason?" I asked.

Her eyes locked on mine, and a charge of something I craved ran through me. It had been so long, but the chemistry I felt when I was around Amelia made me want so much more.

She didn't answer but stood with the wet towels.

"Okay. You're sure about this?"

Her lip curled slightly on the left in a cute smirk, and she nodded. "Ready as I'll ever be."

I drew a breath and unbuttoned my jeans, shoving them over my butt.

"Oh, a briefs guy," she teased.

"Seriously?" I looked over my shoulder.

"Come on. Get the briefs down too."

I rolled my eyes, loving every second of being with Amelia.

"Do you realize that even with being bitten on my thumb and my ass, I haven't had this much fun on a date?" And that was the sad fact of my dating life. *I'm standing here with a thumb and a butt cheek throbbing, and it's better than any other date.*

She snorted. "Please tell me you're kidding."

I shook my head, shoving the waistband of my briefs down just enough under the bite so I didn't reveal too much cheek.

"It might hurt," she muttered, bending over. "But we've got to make sure it's clean."

I nodded as her fingers gently began rubbing the fang marks. She dabbed the wound several times and sighed. "Okay. And now for the bad part."

She reached for the bottle of alcohol and squirted it several times. "How are you doing?"

"Stings, but totally fine." I stared at the fridge, wondering how I would ever explain this date to my cousin.

I wouldn't.

"You're good as new." She took a step back, and I pulled my underwear up, along with my jeans. "Unless, of course, infection sets in, and then you'll need to see Dr. Stan immediately."

I chuckled. "Ah, I'm looking forward to that on date two."

She pressed her lips together and glanced around the kitchen. "So, should we maybe do a raincheck?"

Looking around the kitchen for Oscar, I shook my

head. "I don't think I should leave you alone here."

I pulled out a seat and sat down but shot right up.

"Little sore?"

I shook my head. "Nah."

"I've got the perfect idea." She walked over to the freezer and opened it up. "My brother's got any kind of frozen pizza you can imagine, jalapeno poppers, corndogs, and mozzarella sticks." She turned to look at me. "How about we stay in tonight and load up on junk food? I can prop you up on the couch with pillows and cordon off Oscar from coming into the family room."

"It sounds like heaven."

She smiled and nodded more to herself than to me. "Amazing."

CHAPTER THIRTEEN

Amelia

The one thing that drove me nuts about myself was the inability to keep a straight face. It didn't matter if my life depended on keeping my giggles in. They'd find a way to sneak out.

And here, on my first date since my fiancé dumped me, the guy gets attacked by my brother's cat not once but twice, and I can't keep it together?

I pulled the tray out with two individual pizzas, corndogs, and mozzarella sticks. We didn't want to be complete oinkers, so we didn't cook the poppers this round.

"Anything I can help with?" James asked, walking into the kitchen. "Smells delicious."

Just the mere sight of him made my heart flutter. His

eyes connected with mine, and I felt a wave of anticipation run through me.

"You're supposed to be sitting down on the couch," I scolded him.

He walked over and stood only inches behind me. I could feel his energy rolling off his body, and all I wanted to do was accidentally bump into him and have him take me into his arms and kiss me.

Which was absolutely ridiculous because the poor guy was wounded, and this was only our first date.

Or did the ambulance ride count?

Maybe dropping some lunch off for me added to the tally. Or how about the ice cream?

Yeah, this was definitely date three, and I wanted a kiss.

"I'm hungry." He reached around and grabbed a mozzarella stick.

His hand brushed my arm, and goosebumps spread over my skin.

"Good. Because we have plenty to eat." I reached for two plates and handed one to James.

"What's your idea of a perfect night?" he asked as I grabbed a mini pizza and he loaded his plate.

I turned around and smiled thoughtfully, tilting my

head slightly. "It depends on my mood. This is pretty perfect right now."

James' smile widened. "Good to hear."

"But I'd say after a long day working at the antique store, I love getting home and vegging out. Sometimes, I'll take a long bath and spoil myself with cheese and crackers, or other nights, I'll come home and just research all night about whatever pieces we got into the store that piqued my interest." I shrugged, missing my old apartment. "But the place I'm in now doesn't have a tub, so I'm looking forward to finding a place that does."

"Would you like a beer or a soda to top off our trip down junk food alley?" I teased.

"The water I have from earlier is fine." He nodded as we made our way into the family room.

"Here, let me hold your plate while you get situated," I suggested when he got to the couch.

"I got it." James shook his head and sat down. "Enjoy your food."

I noticed him lifting his one side and maneuvering more onto the pillows.

"I'm so sorry about Oscar." I reached for the remote and turned on the movie we'd picked earlier.

"It's not your fault."

"It kind of is." I shook my head, sitting on the couch next to him. "I never should have agreed to watch Oscar. Someone always gets hurt."

"Speaking of, how are your knuckles?" He took a sip of water.

I glanced at the pink skin, shrugged, and took a bite of pizza. "Probably better than your thumb and rear."

He laughed, shaking his head, and I couldn't help but notice the dark hair tumbling just below his ear. I wanted to brush it back.

"This is really nice. I can't tell you how long it's been since I've been able to watch something that wasn't animated."

I smiled, glancing at him. Most of the time, he'd look at me in a way that said he was feeling the same way I did, and then every so often, like now, I felt like I might be in the friend zone.

Or was I just so damaged that I couldn't even read men anymore?

A sigh slipped out of my lips, and he turned to look at me.

"Everything okay? Am I eating too loudly?"

I snorted in surprise, which made him laugh. "No. Not at all. You're a super quiet eater."

"Then what's on your mind?"

Narrowing my eyes on him, I put my plate on the coffee table. "It's been so long since I've been on a date that I'm just getting in my own head. And just merely confessing that to my date is probably doing more harm than good, which then tells me that it's okay if I don't ever date again because I have a job I enjoy and a town I love to live in." My shoulders brushed my ears, and I realized just how tense I felt.

James laughed and nodded, sweeping his hand over mine. "Listen, it sounds like we're both kind of new at this, and it's not like hopping back on a bicycle like my cousin so often reminds me."

I chuckled, feeling some of the tension leave. "I just..."

Stopping myself, I drew a deep breath.

"You can tell me anything." His eyes stayed on mine, and I suddenly felt like he was telling me the truth.

"There are moments when I wonder if you're here with me because you feel bad about what happened with hanging up on me or if you're here with me because you're actually interested."

James' gaze studied mine, but he didn't say anything.

"Because I'm not into being a pity partner." I licked my lips and waited for him to say something, anything.

He set his plate down, took a drink of water, and turned to look at me. His blue eyes darkened as his lips curled into an incredible smile.

"Then we might be a perfect match because I don't hand out sympathy much." His deep voice stirred something inside me, and he didn't take his eyes off mine. The electricity between us charged at an unstoppable voltage.

I swallowed hard and watched as he stood slowly and turned to face me. He took a step to my end of the couch and smiled. I felt like I was back in seventh grade about to have my first kiss with a crush I'd daydreamed about for months.

James moved his arms to each side of my shoulders, caging me in as he lowered.

My heart rate rose with each passing second as he kept focused on me. The temperature of my body increased tenfold as he stood above me with his mouth so close to mine.

If he were any closer, he could probably feel my heartbeat.

"You're beautiful, funny, vivacious, smart." He smiled wider, but his gaze bored into me. "And sexy as hell."

"Thank you," I squeaked out, which made him shake his head.

"You have nothing to thank me for," he whispered, bringing his lips even closer to mine. "But I apologize for ever making you wonder what my intentions were with this date."

What he didn't know was that no man had ever complimented me like that. I'd become used to hearing all my faults and weaknesses in relationships.

This…this was different.

This was nice.

I closed my eyes, and he brought his mouth to mine and shattered any worries that had built up. His soft lips felt incredible and churned something inside me that I'd never felt before.

His kisses made my body feel weightless under him as his mouth parted. The need behind his kiss built as every cell in my body lit up like fireworks on the Fourth of July.

He moved his fingers through my hair as I looped my arms around his neck.

I felt him smile through our kisses, which made my tummy tighten in need. The thought that I could make him smile made me feel even more euphoric.

He slowly broke our kiss, and I found myself panting softly, but I didn't want this to end.

James picked me up, and I couldn't help but giggle as he spun me around and sat back down, but now I was on his lap.

I braced myself as my legs straddled his lap, and I

pressed my forehead against his.

"Are you sure this is okay with the bite and everything?" I teased as his eyes never strayed, stirring desire through me.

"All I can feel is you, Amelia, and it's all I've wanted to feel since we met." His gaze stayed on mine.

I brought in a slow breath as his eyes dropped to my mouth.

"Now are you starting to understand how I feel about you? What my intentions are?" He traced his thumb along my bottom lip, and I swore that felt even more sensual than our kiss.

But as I sat on his lap, feeling him underneath me, I couldn't help but want more.

So.

Much.

More.

Which was a terrifying relief because I never expected to feel this again. Not since my fiancé crushed my heart into a billion pieces. But I couldn't shake the worry that it could happen to me all over again.

I'd give my heart to someone who doesn't know what to do with it.

I smiled, nodding. "A little bit."

He growled softly with a smile and spread his fingers through my hair, cupping the back of my head and pulling me down until our lips met.

His mouth demanded something from me that I was more than happy to give. He parted my lips with his tongue, and my body molded into his as I let out a little moan of pleasure.

His fingers slid under the hem of my shirt, and my body warmed from his touch.

When I thought it couldn't get any better, his phone rang. We broke our kiss as he quickly dug into his pocket, and I could feel something had changed—something was wrong.

"Sorry. This is Nina's ringtone. I gotta grab it." He pulled out his phone, and I rolled off his lap while nodding in agreement.

He answered the call, and I immediately saw a change. He straightened, and concern washed over his features.

"What happened?" James' gaze became steely as he stared straight ahead.

I could hear the female on the other end of the phone, but I couldn't hear what she was saying.

"Slow down. Okay. You're fine. You're doing good. He's going to be okay." James stood while still on the phone and paced. "Where are they taking him?"

His son?

Oh, no.

My mouth went dry, and I shot up from the couch while my heart raced as I searched James' face for any sign or hint about what was going on.

"I'll be there as fast as I can." He hung up, and his eyes met mine before heading to the door. I was right on his tail. "I have to meet Nina and Henry at the ER."

"What happened? Is everything okay? Will a ferry get you there in time?"

He turned around at the front door and smiled. "They're actually here on the island. I might be one of those helicopter parents or whatever people call us, but I had them hang out at my grandparents' estate…just in case."

I reached for my jacket. "Call your parenting what you will. It's good that you did."

He opened the front door, and I followed. "So, they're at this hospital?"

"Yup."

"I'll come." Before he had a chance to object, I took the keys from him and made my way to his vehicle.

"I know the back roads to the hospital."

He climbed in the passenger seat and nodded, rubbing

his forehead. "My poor little man."

"Don't blame yourself." I turned on the Jeep and backed out of my brother's driveway. "It's going to be okay."

He nodded. "No. It is. You're right. I could just hear him crying in the background, and it absolutely killed me."

I shook my head slowly, driving down the windy road to bypass any traffic. "I can't even imagine."

"This is why I just stay home." He laughed nervously and stared out the window.

"I get it."

I wanted to ask what happened, but I didn't know what degree of injury or accident we were dealing with.

"He was trying to get a cookie out of a cookie jar my cousin brought with her. Somehow, he climbed onto the counter, slid off, and the cookie jar hit his foot and broke."

"Oh, no." I was silently relieved it wasn't worse.

When the back of the hospital came into view, James straightened in the seat. "That's Nina's car right there."

I drove him up to the ER entrance and dropped him off. "I'll be right in. It's probably my uncle who's on duty again."

He gave a quick nod, shut the door, and ran through the sliding doors of the hospital.

Before finding a parking spot, I let out the breath I'd

been holding in and rested my head on the steering wheel as everything from the last fifteen minutes rewound in my head.

The kiss.

The passion.

The worry.

The fear.

James was obviously an amazing dad, and the fact that his son was on the same island, just in case, made my heart melt a little more.

I didn't know enough about his past to understand what had made him so cautious or cynical about life, but I'd imagine being abandoned by your own mom and then having the same thing happen to your son only made him even more jaded about the world we lived in.

I lifted my head up and sighed before driving to a parking spot not far from the door.

As I walked into the ER department, I made my way past admitting and went through the double doors where I heard a little boy sniffling, and my heart ached as I saw his dad kneeling next to him to comfort him.

CHAPTER FOURTEEN

James

Henry's tiny arms wrapped around my neck as we both sat on the hospital bed. He'd been given acetaminophen already, and it would probably be only a matter of time before he drifted to sleep despite the pain.

"I'm so sorry," Nina said for the tenth time, clutching her chest and shaking her head.

"It's not your fault. These little tykes are sneaky and quick. You did the best you could." I nuzzled Henry's hair with my chin, and he giggled in between sniffles.

"I just can't believe it. Everything happened so fast."

The curtain slid open, and Amelia dashed in, looking wild and anxious. "Has my uncle been in yet?"

I nodded. "He ordered an X-ray of his foot, and the nurse already cleaned out the wound."

She instantly looked like a weight had been lifted. "Thank goodness. Okay."

Nina's eyes locked on mine, and a faint smirk spread across her lips, which I ignored. She spun around and stuck out her hand. "You must be Amelia."

Amelia smiled. "That's me in my typical disheveled mess of a being."

"If this is your version of a mess, you don't want to see mine." She smiled. "My cousin was so looking forward to your date. I'm so sorry for blowing it."

Amelia shook her head and flushed. "Oh, no. You didn't. These things happen when you have littles. I'm just relieved it was only a cookie jar incident."

Nina smiled and nodded, keeping her gaze on Amelia. I couldn't guess whether she was giving her the once-over or was genuinely interested in who finally made me step a foot out of my house.

"Who's dat?" Henry asked, pointing in Amelia's direction.

Amelia waved and cocked her head slightly. "I'm a friend of your daddy's."

Henry frowned. "He doesn't have friends."

Nina snickered, and I rolled my eyes. "Thanks, kiddo."

"Well, we can count me as his first, then." Amelia's eyes stayed on mine, and she smiled.

Henry kept staring at her, but this time, he had a big grin. "Pretty."

"Okay, folks. It's X-ray time. We need everyone out and—" Amelia's Uncle walked into the room. "Amelia, what are you doing here? What did you hurt this time? I can only see one patient at a time."

She chuckled and shook her head. "I just drove James here. It's his son who's the patient."

Dr. Stan looked at me and then Amelia before glancing at Nina as the X-ray technician came in.

"I'm just his cousin," Nina added.

The doctor ran his fingers across his chin and nodded. "Okay, everyone out. Dad, you can help little Henry get organized, and then we can just step outside the glass wall while the tech takes a quick picture of his foot. Sound good?"

Henry's breath caught in his throat as he noticed everyone leaving, and before I could stop it, he let out a huge wail.

"It's okay. They aren't going anywhere." I pointed at the glass. "See? Nina and Amelia are right there."

The tech helped me get his leg situated as I kept running my hands across his head to calm his cries down.

"You're such a brave boy," I whispered, hugging him.

"And here is the superhero cape," the tech announced, unfolding the tiny apron that acted as a shield.

That was my cue. I quickly exited as the tech shut the glass door, adjusted the portable machine, took a picture, and all before Henry even looked up from the cape to see we'd all been outside the room.

The tech opened the door. "All done."

We all filed back in, and Henry's red, puffy eyes lit up as he reached out to me.

And I realized all that mattered was him and his little heart. Just like it had been last year and the year before that.

Amelia was impossibly sexy and alluring.

She was incredible in every sense, but she wasn't Henry, and I needed to think of him first.

Always.

"Hey, Buddy," Amelia said softly, touching his little hand that had wrapped around my neck. "You're a brave little Edward."

"Not Edward. I'm Henry."

I chuckled and squeezed him. "Your name is Henry Edward. She was right."

"Oh, yeah." Henry's body relaxed in mine as I slid underneath him and held him on the bed.

Amelia's uncle came into the room. "We don't have the official report from the radiologist, but I can see a fracture on the images."

Nina gulped a cry. "I gave him his first break."

Amelia reached for her hand and shook her head. "You didn't. It was the cookie jar's fault."

Nina looked reassured by Amelia's words and glanced over at me.

"There isn't much to be done other than to stabilize it." Dr. Stan looked over at his niece and crinkled his nose. "Didn't you just break your toe at Christmas?"

"That was two Christmases ago, and it was the big toe, not the pinky."

Dr. Stan shook his head. "It's hard to keep track of you. Okay, I'll have the nurse bring everything in, and I'll be back to tape it up."

Amelia nodded and softly rubbed Henry's back as he continued to loosen up.

"James, I'm so sorry." Nina came over to me and shook her head. "You'll probably never let me watch him again."

I chuckled and nodded. "It's not that. I just don't think

I'll be leaving my house ever until he's eighteen."

Amelia laughed, but I wasn't sure if she could tell whether I was kidding or not.

And I wasn't sure I was, honestly.

I drew a deep breath and let out a slow sigh as I heard Henry's breathing shift.

He fell asleep, but I noticed Amelia continued to rub his back.

These were things I shouldn't be noticing.

Tonight was a stark reminder of why I didn't let myself get involved.

"Hey, you can go home if you want. They'll be finishing up with him soon, and Nina can just drop you off at your brother's." I forced the words out.

She shook her head. "This place is like my second home. I don't want you two alone. Besides, I'll make sure the service level stays where it should."

I studied the kindness in Amelia's eyes and wondered if she was like this to everyone. After all, she went to all the trouble to track me down and hand me letters that I had no plan to ever read.

But that kiss we shared earlier...

It was the hottest kiss I'd ever experienced, and all I could think about was having her fit against me again. I dragged my gaze away from Amelia's, and Nina caught the look in my eyes. She raised her brows.

"Actually, I need to catch the last ferry back over, so I should leave now. No time to drop her off." Nina looked at Amelia. "No offense."

Amelia smiled. "None taken. Ferry schedules dictate life on the islands."

Nina slid me a sly smile, and I knew exactly what she'd be reporting back to her brother.

"It was great meeting you, Amelia." Nina gave Amelia a quick hug and pecked a kiss on top of Henry's head. "I owe him college. You know I'm good for it."

She gave a quick wave and ducked out just as Dr. Stan came in with one of the nurses. "Oh, good. I'm glad to see our little patient is getting some shut-eye. That should make this easier."

"So, I see this is the fellow you're not dating but keeps magically appearing in the emergency room with you." Dr. Stan peered over his spectacles at his niece.

Her teeth tugged on her bottom lip in a seriously sexy way as she debated what to say and glanced over at me. She caught me staring, and her cheeks flushed.

"We might be dating," she said as I helped turn Henry over and adjusted his leg.

"Well, good. You need to get the bad taste out of your mouth from that creep you kept trying to pass off as husband material. Come on over to our house tomorrow, James. We have a lunch planned that usually goes right into dinner." He started taping my son's toes while talking, and I noticed Amelia's eyes widen. "Don't you think that would be great?" Dr. Stan peered at his niece.

"Uh—" Amelia nearly choked on her mumble and looked over at me.

"I'm not sure Henry will feel up to it."

"Kids are resilient," Dr. Stan continued. "Besides, my wife makes fresh ice cream with June raspberries. Blink, and you'll miss it. Right, Amelia?"

I looked over at Amelia, who looked somewhat comatose.

"Right. Yeah. Good stuff. We'd love to have you." She nodded.

"Well, I'd planned on staying at the orchard anyway, so if you're sure we won't be an imposition."

"Not at all. Fresh blood is always welcome. Hearing about the antique store every family gathering can be…" He looked at Amelia. "Let's just say I'd love to hear about whatever it is you've got going on in your life."

I laughed and shook my head as Amelia seemed to

relax.

Dr. Stan worked quickly and gently on my son's toe with barely a stir from Henry and without even realizing it, Amelia was stroking my back as Dr. Stan finished up.

I wasn't sure she even realized she was providing that comfort, but when Dr. Stan finished, he smiled at me and nodded. "When he's awake, keep ice on it for ten to fifteen minutes every few hours. I'll make sure to have some fresh packs tomorrow. And Amelia, fill him in on our address for some of that raspberry ice cream. I'm sure Henry will love it. The nurse will be in with written instructions."

And with that, Dr. Stan left Amelia and me alone in the room with my sleeping Henry.

"Listen, I didn't want to be rude to your uncle, but I don't have to come tomorrow. I know you weren't expecting that."

She nodded with a smile. "No. I think it's good."

"You sure? Because you looked like you swallowed a goose egg when your uncle mentioned it."

Amelia laughed softly. "I just kind of panicked because I can only imagine what my family will put you through. There will be questions and assumptions and just all kinds of things most people can't prepare for."

There she goes again, worrying about someone else.

Amelia drew in a deep breath. "And I'll be sure to make sure that the family knows not to refer to us as anything but friends. I don't want Henry to get confused."

And again.

"Wow." I nodded slowly. "I appreciate that. Really. I do."

"But since he's sleeping…" She smiled and a sweet look dashed across her face. "I wanted to tell you how much I enjoyed spending time with you tonight. It's been a long time."

Her words felt like my own, but all I could do was nod as I wondered what more I could give, what more I should give.

Because the last thing I wanted to do was hurt Amelia.

CHAPTER FIFTEEN

Amelia

I'd changed my clothes three different times and still felt like a hot mess. I'd braided my hair, taken it down, put it up in a ponytail, and even curled it before slapping it into a bun and calling it quits.

I shouldn't care what I looked like because it was just a casual family get together.

With the guy I was desperately falling for.

It didn't help that I saw the way he was with his son. It was like he turned into one big gooey marshmallow of a man around his little boy, and I couldn't eat it up fast enough.

And his little boy.

They don't make them any cuter.

However, all of this was supposed to be for me to

slowly explore and unravel and run away from without my entire family being involved.

Now I had to navigate this unfamiliar territory in front of a regular walking, talking peanut gallery. My only saving grace was that Brad and his buddies were in the middle of Montana.

I let out a quick breath and dabbed some lip gloss on before heading out the door. My aunt and uncle didn't actually live too far away from the infamous apple orchard where James and his son were staying.

I thought about offering to pick them up, but I didn't want to put that pressure on any of us. Plus, he might want to escape with his son before I could, and I'd be in the car I'd borrowed from my parents, which obviously doesn't have a car seat.

Wow. To think I just worried about having a car seat for little Henry.

I needed to slow down. Just because that kiss nearly caught me on fire doesn't mean that we're in a relationship. It's too soon to even call it that, especially with his son. We needed to take things slow.

Today would be good. A nice break for everyone, and if Henry needed any other attention, at least my uncle was there to check on his toe.

I climbed in the car, rolled the windows down, and took off down the winding road that led along the island. The deep blue water stretched as far as the eye could see, and I felt lighter than I had in a long time.

A really long time, and I didn't just mean from my car breaking and my apartment going up in flames. This was the soul-crushing, heart-shattering type of weight slowly unwrapping its tentacles from my chest and letting me exhale.

But I still knew better than to rush anything. We'd only shared one kiss.

And that kiss only happened to straighten out any misunderstandings surrounding intention.

It seemed like his intentions were on the right track. I smiled to myself as I thought back to the look in his eyes as he boxed me in and brought his sweet lips to mine. My stomach swirled at the thought.

When I pulled down my aunt and uncle's long driveway, I was surprised to see James already ducking into his Jeep to pull Henry from the backseat.

My heart literally sputtered at the sight of him when he held his son on his hip and glanced in my direction.

James wore a pair of low slung cargo shorts and a navy Polo, and he'd dressed his son in the same outfit.

My heart tugged even more at the sight.

I slowly pulled next to them and parked. James smile widened as I climbed out of the car.

"It's not too late for me to flee," he teased.

I laughed and shook my head. "That would only raise suspicions. And also, I did text everyone to be considerate of labels."

"Ah, gotcha. Thanks for that."

I turned my attention to Henry who had his head resting on his dad's chest.

"How are you doing?"

"Good."

"Glad to hear it." I smiled at the spitting image of James and shook my head. "He's a cutie."

"I'm glad you said it because sometimes I wonder if I'm just biased."

I chuckled as we walked up to the entry of my aunt and uncle's home.

Without even ringing the doorbell, my uncle opened the door and ushered us in.

"How's my little patient?" he asked Henry.

"Good."

James laughed and glanced at me. "He's a man of few words."

I shrugged. "Nothing wrong with that. It's something

my brother could take a cue from."

"Is he going to be here?" my uncle asked.

"No. He's still in Montana with his friends."

We followed my uncle down the hallway to the great room overlooking the water. "I don't even want to know what he's up to."

"Me neither." I nodded, glancing at Henry, quietly taking everything in.

"Thanks again for inviting my son and me over."

"I'm delighted you could make it. Is it time for some ice on his foot?"

Henry nodded, and James laughed. "Apparently it is."

"Right this way. I'll show you where we keep them."

I watched the men wander into the kitchen as my aunt snuck up behind me.

"I bet this time last year, you never would have believed you'd be here with that man. Am I right?" Her elbow dug into my side, and I wiggled away.

"Let's not get carried away. We're just friends, remember?"

"I get it. I get it. There's a child involved."

I rolled my eyes. "We've only been on one date and that was cut short."

"Not what I've heard," she hummed, and I wondered

who in my family had been blabbing.

I looked over to see Henry with a scoop of ice cream on a cone carefully walking while trying not to hurt his pinky toe.

"He didn't want to be carried," James explained still holding the ice.

"This is Aunt Carrie," I said.

"Pleasure meeting you."

My aunt beamed. "Pleasure is all mine. I heard you rode in the ambulance when Amelia fell down the stairs. So sweet of you. Most men get scared away from someone who's so accident prone."

"Thanks for that, Aunt Carrie."

James laughed. "I'm used to it with a toddler around the house. I'll just have to remember to do better at babyproofing my house if she comes over."

"Very funny."

I heard a ruckus at the front door and saw my cousin coming in with her husband and two kids. Elizabeth was six years younger than me, but she seemed to have her life far more put together than I did.

"Hey, Amelia." She grinned and then stopped in her tracks when she saw who was standing next to me. "What's he doing here?"

My aunt and I traded glances as James bit his bottom lip and pulled his son into him.

"He's my guest. Why? Do you two know one another?" I asked.

"You should ask him." She smirked as her two toddlers each grabbed a leg and spun down to her ankles.

I turned to James. "Is there something I should know about you and Elizabeth?"

"She dated my cousin Lucas."

"Before I met Pete," she explained, glancing at me. "And this one decided to do Lucas' dirty work."

My brows knitted together. "Dirty work?"

"It wasn't my finest hour," James said as he bent over and picked up Henry.

"That's your son?" she asked.

"He is." James nodded proudly, but I was too nosy about the history here. "This is Henry."

"So, what did you do to my cousin?"

"Lucas wanted to break up with her, but he didn't want to hurt her feelings and he felt that I had no feelings, so unbeknownst to me, he had me break up with her on his behalf."

"Seriously?" I glanced at my cousin, who nodded. "When was this?"

"Like seven or eight years ago." She shrugged. "But I can't hold too much of a grudge since I met Pete that night."

"Really?" I asked, not sure how I knew none of this.

"Yup. I had drowned my sorrows in too many tequila shots, and Pete made sure I made it home safely."

"Well, good. I'm glad all is well." I chuckled and shook my head.

"Do you want to go on the play equipment?" Elizabeth asked her kids.

Henry perked up at the mention, and James slid him down to the floor, and he quickly followed my cousin and her kids.

"Apparently, he didn't need ice." James laughed.

"You've got to tell me how you broke up with someone you weren't even going with." I raised my brows as we slowly made it outside to see Henry hobbling around, following Elizabeth's kids.

"I told her the truth. It wasn't working out between Lucas and her, and it's probably better for her sake because my cousin was an ass."

"And then what happened?"

Elizabeth turned around and laughed. "I agreed with him and walked up to the bar where I spent most of the night."

"Why did you agree to do that to her?" I folded my

arms over my chest and stared at him.

"I didn't actually agree to it. Lucas was supposed to meet me for drinks with Elizabeth coming too, and as we were sitting there together, I started getting texts from Lucas after he didn't show up."

"I did kind of coerce James to tell me what was going on." She shrugged.

"Yeah. It wasn't like I got joy out of relaying the news," he added, glancing at me.

"Well, at least it tells me I'm not as screwed up as I thought."

My cousin chuckled and James shook his head.

"Do you want to go down to the beach?" I asked James.

He glanced at his boy, and Elizabeth smiled, nodding. "It's okay. I'll watch him. Go check out the beach. It's really pretty."

I flashed my cousin a grateful smile, and she nodded as James' hand slowly moved down my spine. We started toward the water, and I wondered how things felt so easy with James. With my ex, I always felt like I wasn't good enough or my family was too in everyone's business around him, but with James, everything felt natural.

I clenched my jaw and gave myself a friendly PSA.

This was all new with James and could be gone by tomorrow. I needed to chill and focus on the here and now.

Like my aunt and uncle's beautiful yard with a play area for the grandkids and a sprawling grassy area that led to a hill overlooking the water.

We reached the edge of the grass and started down the wooden steps dug into the hill that led toward the rocky beach below. The gentle sound of lapping waves grew as we moved down the hill.

"For the record, I don't do anyone's dirty work anymore." He sounded adorable.

I turned around and smiled at James. "Good to know. Your cousin sounds like a character."

"Oh, he is." He shook his head. "That first night I met you, he had convinced me and Henry to go with him to be his wingmen."

I laughed as I hopped off the last step to the pebble-filled beach. "Nothing like using a toddler as a right-hand man to pick up women."

James chuckled and nodded, standing next to me and looking at the inky-blue water snaking its way to shore and back out. "But he's one of the few family members I have." He looked at me. "And he's pretty much my best friend."

"I'm sure my brother and your cousin would be fast

friends, so it's not like I can say too much."

Even though it was June, a cool breeze brushed against my skin, and I shivered.

James brought me into him as we slowly walked along the rocky beach closer to the water.

"I've been replaying last night in my head over and over again," he said softly as I rested my head on his chest.

"I bet. I have too. The thought of something happening to poor Henry nearly killed me. I'm just grateful it was only a cookie jar incident." I looked up into his gaze, and his grin widened.

"I was actually talking about our kiss."

Chuckling, I looped my arm around his waist. "Oh, right. Yeah. That too."

He brushed his lips over my forehead as I drew a breath.

"It felt nice," I lied. It felt more than nice. It felt like I couldn't breathe. It felt like I was flying high and free. Just the thought of his lips on mine made my skin flush and heat pool in the bottom of my belly.

His eyes stayed on mine, and I could tell he had more to say.

"I'm worried I might not be able to give you what you need," he finally said.

My heart sputtered. "I don't know what I need."

James nodded, and his blue eyes reflected the sunlight bouncing off the water. "You need a man who puts you first. One hundred percent."

"Okay."

"I don't know if I can do that."

I loosened my arms around his waist and nodded. "I appreciate your honesty."

"It's just with Henry, he's my number one. That's the least I can do for him."

"I completely agree."

"You do?" His gaze searched mine.

"He will always be your priority. That's how it should be." I shook my head. "I would be worried if he wasn't."

I glanced at a boulder a few feet away and made my way over and sat down.

He took a seat next to me and slid his hand on my knee. "I just don't want to over promise anything."

"Then don't." My stomach was twisting in knots. Was this where he broke things off before they even got started?

"But I don't want to stay away from you." James looked me dead in the eye and then tugged me up from the boulder.

He closed the gap between us, and my heart fluttered.

"It sounds like you're as confused as I am."

James smiled and nodded slowly as his hand slid up my spine and tangled through my hair.

His gaze darkened with the same desire I felt last night, and he pulled my mouth to his. He kissed me softly, teasing me with every sweep of his tongue until all my worries drifted away for another day.

CHAPTER SIXTEEN

James

The softness of her lips made it hard to concentrate on much until I heard clapping above us. We parted, and I noticed her sister Emily grinning at us.

A little blush crawled up Amelia's cheeks as we stepped back from each other, but I grabbed her hand and held it tight.

She squeezed it back.

"Lunch will be ready in about ten minutes," she shouted down the hill.

"Thanks," Amelia said, laughing.

"Anytime." Her sister walked away, and I pulled Amelia back into my arms.

"You feel good," I whispered, bringing my lips close

to hers.

She nodded. "You do too. What does this mean?"

"It means I want to keep seeing you."

"I want that too," she whispered, glancing toward the water.

"But things with me will be complicated. They have to be with my son."

She nodded and brought her eyes to mine. "I know we don't know where this will go, but I haven't dated anyone since my ex."

The fear in her eyes pummeled through me. I couldn't break this girl. She'd already been broken once.

"Same." My jaw tensed thinking back to Henry's mom. I didn't want Henry to grow up like I did, skeptical of anything and everyone.

But Amelia had this innocence about her that drew me to her, and part of me wanted to believe that she was different. That she wouldn't run like everyone always did.

"Should we go get lunch?" she asked.

I kept her hand in mine as we made our way up the wooden stairs. The sounds of laughter and children giggling floated through the air. More people had obviously showed up, and I realized I might be meeting all of her family.

Amelia reached the top step and gulped a squeak. I

nearly bumped into her when I saw what made her stop in her tracks.

"Lucas," I muttered under my breath.

"Emily and Elizabeth." Amelia looked over her shoulder at me with wide eyes.

"Well, this lunch just got a whole lot more interesting."

She laughed. "Maybe we can snatch Henry and flee."

Lucas spotted us and grinned with a big wave, but I couldn't muster a smile.

Not now.

Just when I thought I had a handle on things, Lucas and his past showed up to screw with my present. I could only imagine the drama that could overtake this family lunch.

"You okay?" Amelia asked.

"Yeah. Just hoping Lucas doesn't mess up my chances with you," I admitted.

"He can't be that bad."

I laughed and shook my head. "Depends on the day."

"Hey, Mom." Amelia walked over to her parents, and I stayed a couple of steps behind as Henry noticed me and darted toward me.

"Love your new friends?" I asked him.

"Yes. The best." I lifted Henry into my arms and

walked over to Amelia's parents.

"Hey, sweetie. I'm so glad you invited James." Her mom smiled at me and glanced at her husband.

"Mom, we're just friends." Her eyes stayed focused on her parents.

"Oh, of course." Her dad nodded and reached out a hand.

"We haven't had a formal introduction. I'm Theo. My wife's name is Cynthia. It's good to meet you, James. Your boy is a really special little man."

I swelled inside. There was just something about other people taking the time to notice how incredible my son was that made me soften a little toward the human race.

"I'm a lucky father."

"Did you hear the gossip about Emily's date?" her mom whispered. "He dated Elizabeth. Crazy."

I bit my lip and glanced at Amelia, who snickered. "What's even crazier is that Lucas and James are cousins."

Henry wiggled out of my arms and dashed over to his new friends as Lucas and Emily wandered over.

Emily grimaced. "Well, that was awkward over there. What are the odds? I've never seen Elizabeth so snippy before."

Amelia eyed me as Lucas looked like he'd seen a

ghost, and I guess, in a way, he had.

Theo and Cynthia looked bemused as Lucas ran his index finger along his collar.

"Lunch is ready." Amelia's aunt wandered toward us with a smile. "And don't eat too much. I churned fresh raspberry ice cream."

"Mae and Audrey are going to be so annoyed they got today's shift. They love Aunt Carrie's ice cream."

I stood in awe at the simplicity and adoration of family that surrounded me. There weren't ulterior motives. They were just gathered together because they enjoyed each other's company.

Dr. Stan walked over to the table with a platter of sandwiches and spun around. "My island-famous pork sliders."

Everyone drifted over to the buffet table, grabbed plates, filled up, and settled around a longer table. I made Henry's plate, putting extra pickles on the side, and wandered over to Amelia. Henry had already claimed the seat next to her.

I refused to read anything into it. He was three.

"So, word around town is that the old orchard is opening up for fall?" Dr. Stan asked before taking a bite of potato salad.

I smiled, always amazed at how quickly word traveled around small towns, even more so on the islands. "That's true."

Lucas straightened and nodded his head, hoping to redeem some points. "Yeah. James, Nina, and I are heading up the festival. We hope to make it as grand as in years past."

"Well, you'll have a lot of community support," Dr. Stan said, glancing at Amelia's mom. "Lots of good memories there."

"Indeed," Cynthia agreed. "It would be nice to have something to look forward to in the fall that the little ones can enjoy."

"Don't you two have a bit of a sordid history at the apple fest?" Emily's brows arched.

"All a misunderstanding," Amelia said, laughing. "I thought he was making fun of Mae. Turns out he was just trying to tell her she had a piece of red apple peel in her braces."

"Remember that one year there were pony rides?" Emily asked, glancing at her parents.

"How can we forget? Amelia fell off on the first lap."

I laughed and snuck my hand on top of Amelia's under the table.

"Well, we should add pony rides to the list of

entertainment," Lucas said, nodding.

He was obviously trying to earn brownie points.

A sharp pain in my rear jolted me forward, and Amelia glanced at me. "You okay?"

"Yeah. Fine."

She scowled. "Are you sure?"

Truth be told, my ass cheek had developed a bit of throbbing pain this morning, and I kept hoping it would go away.

"Totally fine."

"Daddy's butt hurts," Henry exclaimed, shoveling in another bite of potato salad.

The table fell silent and all eyes turned toward me. I laughed and shook my head. "It's nothing. Really."

"Have a case of 'rhoids?" Dr. Stan asked. His expression turned serious while Lucas did everything in his power to keep himself together.

"Uh, no. Thanks for asking. I'm fine in that department." I laughed, shaking my head.

Dr. Stan wiped his mouth with a napkin and nodded. It was so quiet around the table, you could hear the waves lapping against the rocks a hundred feet away.

"Well, they can be a real nuisance. I diagnose at least three cases a week in the ER."

"Nope. Never been an issue," I assured him.

I looked down at Henry whose grin reached from one side of his face to the other.

"Oscar bit him," Amelia announced.

And now I wasn't sure who I could trust. It was like Amelia and Henry were already on the same team.

Dr. Stan scowled. "Where?"

"That damn cat," Amelia's mom muttered.

"His butt," Henry announced before he erupted into giggles.

"Your butt?" Lucas scrunched his face.

"Honestly, I'm fine. But I do appreciate everyone's concern."

And even if I weren't, I'd will it that way.

"Nonsense. You've got a licensed practitioner at your fingertips. Cat bites can be nasty. Let's have a look. You don't need an infection to spread."

Lucas nodded. "For sure."

"How did Oscar bite your butt?" Emily asked, cocking her head slightly.

"Long story," Amelia said. "But his fangs went through his jeans."

Her sister winked at me. "Ah, that's what I was wondering."

Amelia pursed her lips. "I'm sure it was."

Her parents chuckled.

"Come on. It'll be quick." Dr. Stan was already up.

I glanced at my cousin before standing. "I'll be right back, Henry."

As I followed Amelia's uncle into the house, I couldn't understand what I'd done in my life to get me here. Sure, I might not always be the most pleasant of people, but I didn't go out of my way to hurt people.

Yet, here I was, about to bend over in front of my girlfriend's uncle to prove that my ass was fine.

"I see the way you look at my niece." He motioned toward the open door of the powder room. "And I see the way she looks at you."

I nodded, not sure I really wanted to get into it at this particular moment.

"Okay. Where's the bite?"

I moved the waistband of my shorts and boxers down enough to reveal the bite on my cheek.

"Ooh," he hissed. "That's not good."

"Serious?" I glanced over my shoulder.

"Yeah. I'm going to write you a prescription for an oral antibiotic and then an ointment, but I want you to follow up with your primary care physician in three days or go to the emergency room if things get worse."

"Wow. Okay. That wasn't what I was expecting." I adjusted my shorts and followed the doctor to the kitchen where he pulled out his laptop.

"What pharmacy should I send it to? You need to pick up the meds today."

I nodded. "Just the pharmacy here is fine. Whatever it's called."

"They're closed on Sunday, but the hospital pharmacy is open. I'll call and make sure they have it ready for you after I submit it online."

"Thanks, Doctor."

"I have to make sure you're in tip-top shape for my niece. It's been a long time since she's opened herself up."

"Yes, sir."

We walked outside to the patio, and everyone turned to look at us, and I smiled.

"Henry and I should probably get going. Turns out, Oscar did some damage. I need to pick up some meds."

My cousin looked surprised and stood. "I'll drive."

"Are you sure?"

"Emily drove us here. I can drive your car and then you can drop me off at mine."

Emily nodded and stood. "Absolutely. Go help your

cousin."

Elizabeth looked annoyed as Lucas put on his superhero cape, but she kept quiet.

Amelia cupped Henry's hand in hers and walked him over to me. "Do you need any help?"

The thought of saying goodbye to Amelia was rough. It felt like we'd barely gotten to spend much time together, and the kiss only skewed things. We hadn't even talked about when we could see each other again.

Henry tugged on Lucas' shirt, and he picked him up and started toward the house.

"Thanks for such a lovely lunch," I told Amelia's family. "I'm sorry I have to cut it short, but doctor's orders."

"Oscar is a terror. We totally understand." Amelia's mom shook her head.

"I'll walk you out," Amelia said as we made our way into the house. "It was nice seeing you today."

Lucas walked Henry out the front door and shut it behind him.

"Well, I'm not sure how many years it will take to live this down with your family." I laughed. "I'm still trying to work through the trauma of having your uncle look at my ass."

She giggled. "I just always manage to bring out the best in people."

I smiled, running my thumb across her cheek. "And you do."

Amelia let out a wistful sigh.

"If you're not busy later, I'd love to have you stop by the orchard. That's where Henry and I will be."

Her brows raised. "Yeah? You wouldn't mind?"

"I'd be sad if you didn't."

Amelia's cute lips pulled into a smile. "Well, I don't want to make you sad."

"Good. I'll see you in a bit."

She stood on her toes and swept a soft kiss across my cheek. "I'll see you soon."

I didn't want to leave. I wanted to take her in my arms and kiss her again.

But the horn sounded from out front, and I knew I'd better go.

"Thanks for coming," she said, waving as I made my way to the door.

"Thank your aunt and uncle again for me." I laughed. "And for saving my life."

She laughed. "Well, we don't want things to go to his head."

I chuckled as she shut the door behind us, and I poked my head in to check Henry's buckle. He'd already conked out.

I gingerly slid into the passenger seat as Lucas started the engine.

"Can you believe Elizabeth is here? That she's Emily's cousin? How can my luck be so bad?"

"Karma."

Although, I wasn't sure where that put me with the cat bite and all.

As he pulled down the driveway, I thought about Amelia's family. I wasn't even part of the family, but I felt warmth flowing freely, and I couldn't even fathom what the holidays must be like. It wasn't something I'd ever craved, and I never had.

Even though I loved my grandparents, I never felt warmth from them. Sometimes, I felt more like a duty and obligation rather than a grandson.

My mind flicked back to my mother and what Amelia had said.

That she picked up on love from the letter she'd read from my mom. The weird thing was that I thought I'd felt that from my mom too, until I didn't.

The only time I'd felt this kind of warmth was when my mom would hold me and rock me when I was a little kid… before she left. It was such a faint memory, I sometimes wondered if I imagined it, if it even happened at all.

CHAPTER SEVENTEEN

Amelia

"He's a really good sport," my mom whispered, leaning into me. "I can see why you're enamored."

"Yeah. I'm not sure how I haven't scared him off yet. Things haven't exactly been smooth sailing around me."

My mom chuckled and pushed a piece of hair behind my ear. "They never are with you. His little boy is cute."

"He's a doll."

"Are you worried about that?" she asked.

I shrugged. "It's too early to be worried about anything."

But that wasn't true. I was a born worrier. I worried about how James would react to the letters, how he'd react to me being a klutz, or to me wishing he'd read the letters from his mom.

But it wasn't my business. I found them and handed them over. Now, it was up to him to read her words. It was like with the diary too. I didn't read it, but I would save it for him in case he was ever curious. I just worried that day would never come.

"I should get going." I hugged my mom before taking off and found myself worrying all the way to his house.

What if Henry hated me? What if I said the wrong thing in front of him?

As I pulled up to the drive, the large gate slowly swung open, and I drove through.

The perfectly lined orchard looked just like I remembered it from my childhood.

I spotted James' Jeep and pulled next to it. I wasn't sure how long I'd be staying, but it was getting close to dark.

Everything about this estate was in pristine condition. The mansion was immaculate, the gardens tidily bloomed along the paths, and wealth oozed out of every crevice.

Before I had a chance to ring the doorbell, Henry swung open the wide door with his dad coming up behind him.

"Meleeya," Henry exclaimed, wrapping his arms around my leg.

"Hey, Henry." I ruffled the top of his head, and he

giggled before letting go and running back inside.

"I was worried you might not come." James smiled and pulled me in for a quick hug.

"Any chance I have to spend time away from Oscar, I'll take."

He laughed. "Do you ever worry about what he might do to you in your sleep?"

I grabbed his arm and squeezed it. "All the time."

As I walked into the grand house, I realized it looked exactly like I had imagined it since I was a little girl. Ornate furniture dotted the expansive foyer, and intricate wallpaper adorned the hallway. Polished wood floors went in every direction, and each table had been topped with something antique from different periods.

There was a lot on display here, and I was still in the foyer.

"We've left it just as my grandparents had it," James explained.

I nodded, taking it all in. "You're not a floral wallpaper type of guy?"

He smiled and shook his head. "I just made some homemade macaroni and cheese. Would you like some?"

"I'd love some," I confessed as I followed him down a hall into a large great room. Henry was sitting in front of a large marble fireplace with a mountain of colorful wooden blocks.

I followed James into the kitchen, where a large casserole dish overflowing with cheese took center stage on the CornuFé 110 range. The brass knobs and hardware stood out against the navy-blue stove. It was gorgeous, but all I could really appreciate was the mac and cheese.

"It smells amazing," I told him, getting closer to the stove.

James nodded and reached for a plate. "It's one of my specialties."

"I'd be afraid to cook on this stove."

James filled my plate with mac and cheese and smiled, shaking his head. "It's got more bark than bite."

"There are like eight knobs on the thing." I took a bite of the mac and cheese and shut my eyes in heaven.

The man could cook.

"You like it?"

"Love it."

"Okay, so now that I've buttered you up, I have a favor to ask."

"Go for it."

"When my cousin took me to the hospital to pick up the meds, they weren't ready. I just got a call that I can go pick them up, but I don't want to disrupt Henry. He's kind of in his wind-down phase before bed."

My heart stammered, but I could see the pleading look in James' gaze and couldn't say no.

"Sure. Of course."

"Thanks. I'll be right back, and you can call me if you need anything."

I followed James into the family room where Henry was building a castle or spaceship with his blocks, I couldn't exactly tell, and James bent down and kissed the top of Henry's head.

"Amelia is going to look after you for a few minutes while I run and get my medicine."

Henry nodded and didn't seem to really pay attention as his dad darted out of the room. I sat down on the couch and Henry played at my feet. It was much easier than watching Oscar.

Until Henry looked up and glanced around the room.

"Daddy?"

"He'll be right back."

Tears erupted and funneled down Henry's cheeks as the blocks fell from his tiny little hands. "I want Daddy."

I set my plate down and slid on the floor with Henry, pulling him into my arms.

"He'll be right back, love."

He sniffled into my arm as I slowly rocked him and felt his tears go through my shirt.

"Daddy," he sputtered again, but this time not as frantic as I rocked his tiny body.

I closed my eyes as I felt Henry's body relax into mine. I expected him to roll off and start playing blocks again.

Glancing down, I realized his little mouth hung open with his tear-stained cheeks and eyes closed. The little man had fallen asleep in my arms.

I tucked him closer and used my sleeves to wipe his cheeks as his little breaths fell into a steady rhythm.

My neck started to kink, so I reached for a pillow and pulled it onto the floor next to us and slowly slid down, careful not to disturb Henry.

Scooting the blocks away with my feet, I adjusted Henry onto the floor with the pillow, but as soon as I pulled my arm away, his eyes flew open, and garble started coming out of his mouth. He looked fuzzy, like he wasn't really awake, so I slid my arm back under him and settled in. His eyes quickly shut, and he went back to deep, steady breaths.

I stared at the ceiling and noticed there were a few stencils in the corner that matched the molding. There wasn't one place in this house that hadn't been thought about.

As I heard Henry's steady breaths, I started to feel sleepy and shut my eyes just for a few seconds.

It would only be a few seconds.

I heard shuffling and noticed the lights had been shut off. I turned over to see no Henry and realized I was on a bed.

My heart raced. Had I really fallen asleep, and for how long?

And the weirdest part was that I felt the most rested I'd felt in years.

I shot up, shoved off the covers, and made my way to the door that was partially cracked open. I looked up and down the hallway and realized James must have carried me upstairs.

The thought brought a smile to my lips as I stepped into the hallway. I saw a door slightly open at the end of the hall and slowly made my way toward the room. As I got closer, I heard James softly singing, and my heart skipped.

I peered into the bedroom to see Henry in a twin bed and James sitting on the edge, rubbing his son's small back. I melted on the spot seeing the love he had for his son. I could watch this forever.

But I stepped wrong, and the floor creaked.

James looked over his shoulder and smiled at me before bending down and kissing his son.

He slowly made his way over, and we walked quietly

down the hall.

"I thought you'd be out until morning." James smiled when we got to the stairs. "I've never seen someone sleep that soundly aside from Henry."

"That's not usually what happens for me, but I feel like I've had the best sleep in years."

"I was shocked to see Henry asleep when I got home."

"Oh, I'm sorry. Should I have kept him awake?" Shoot. This was why I wasn't good at the parenting thing. I'd put kids to bed when they should be awake and wake them up when they should be sleeping.

James chuckled and shook his head. "No, I mean he has never, and I mean *never*, fallen asleep when someone else watches him."

"Really?" His words warmed my core as I stepped off the last stair step.

"Yeah. It was nice to see."

I chuckled and nodded. "Well, I never intended to fall asleep. Henry got sad when he realized you weren't here, and I held him and then he fell asleep in my arms, but whenever I moved my arm away, he'd wake up startled, so I snuggled next to him."

"You two looked beautiful." He smiled, and I felt my insides twisting into some tangled knot of emotion I wasn't ready for yet.

"Thanks for carrying me upstairs. You must be a strong man."

He rolled his eyes. "The way you were sleeping, I was sure you'd sleep until morning."

"What time is it?"

"It's about one o'clock."

"Wow. I should probably get back to Oscar."

James' expression fell slightly. "It's pretty late to be driving out. You're more than welcome to stay the night."

His eyes stayed on mine, and a wave of emotion washed over me.

"Oscar does have enough food and water," I said softly, warming up to the idea of not leaving.

"Then it's settled." James winked at me.

"But there's a slight problem," I confessed.

"What's that?"

"I'm wide awake."

His smile widened, and he scooped me into his arms. "I think we can find things to do."

The electricity running through us made my knees weak, and my imagination ran wild.

"Oh, yeah, Mister? Like what?"

His arm swooped under me, and I fell into his chest

as he carried me down the hall toward the family room.

The colorful blocks had been put away, the pillows put back in place, and my dirty plate taken away. He really was such a dad, and I couldn't help but fall a little harder.

James set me on the couch, and I wiggled out of his embrace. "What are your plans?"

"I don't have any," he said, letting out a deep breath. "Which in itself is frightening as hell."

I smiled and nodded, running my index finger along his jaw as he leaned over me.

"You're so beautiful, Amelia," he whispered, trailing his mouth down my jaw to my neck.

"Thank you," I muttered into his shoulder as I looped my arms around him.

He chuckled and pulled back. "You don't have to thank me for telling you the truth."

And I realized I'd never been told that before by someone I'd dated, not until James. And this was the second time he told me that.

"I think you're extremely sexy and handsome and kind." I kept my arms looped around his neck.

"Yeah?"

"And I'm scared to death."

He smiled and nodded slowly. "I am too."

"I'm scared to screw up the possibilities, and I'm scared that I might fall hard again, and…"

"What if we don't think about the end and only focus on the beginning?" he asked, sliding his lips against mine.

"Mm-hmm," I said, feeling his lips brush against my skin. "I think I can do that."

He pulled away, and his lips twisted into a sexy grin. "We'll take it slow."

"I can handle that." I looked into his eyes and saw a storm of emotions brewing behind his gaze.

"But if it were completely left up to me, I'd take you upstairs tonight."

"And?" I asked, feeling the heat pooling deep in my belly.

"And explore every single inch of your body with my hands." He kissed me and pulled away. "And then my lips would follow." He kissed me again, and desire pulsed through me like never before.

CHAPTER EIGHTEEN

James

Seeing Henry cradled in Amelia's arms did something to me that I couldn't turn back from. I wanted Henry to have that kind of love so bad it physically hurt. But I also didn't want him to experience it, only to have it taken away like had happened to me. There was no recovering from that type of pain.

I knew I had to tread lightly with this whole situation no matter how much I wanted to sleep with Amelia or fantasize about a future with her.

I thought back to that night where she clutched his little hand when he stirred as I picked him up. It was so instinctive for her, second nature, that she did it in her sleep.

And the beautiful smile of hers as she hugged him

tightly.

But I won't forget her words later that night, "I'm afraid to fall because the last time I did, there was no one around to pick up the pieces." She looked into my eyes after we'd spent hours kissing and exploring each other's bodies and said those words.

It nearly killed me. I understood that more than anyone.

Staying far away from people had become my defense mechanism, and it had worked until Amelia. Now, I didn't want to stay away.

"I said, did you want a golf cart or not?" Lucas brought his brows together.

"Golf cad," Henry said, and I smiled with a nod. We were still working on his Rs. It was a process, a bit of hit and miss.

"You heard the man, Lucas. A golf cart it is."

Lucas spoke to the guy at the counter as Henry stood with his miniature golf clubs.

"You excited?"

Henry nodded and put a sucker in his mouth that Lucas had bought him. Not exactly toddler food.

I bent down and whispered to Henry, "Just do a few licks on it, but don't try to chew it or crunch it. Keep it out of your mouth."

Henry nodded.

I probably went over the top getting Henry all set up with golf clubs at this age, and he'd probably outgrow them by next year, but it was all about the memories. Something I wish I had more of from growing up. Apart from the revolving door of friends from the boarding schools and the shenanigans we'd find ourselves in, I had very few family memories.

"Alright, let's get the show on the road before we miss our tee-time." Lucas snapped his fingers, and I picked up Henry and our golf bags.

As we made our way outside, the sun gleamed brightly and the fir trees lining the fairway swayed gently from a light breeze.

We secured our bags onto the back of the cart, and Lucas sat in the driver's seat. Henry crawled next to him, but I wasn't going to let him be alone up front. He was too short, and all it would take was one of Lucas' goofy moves to have Henry fly out the front.

No. I was definitely sitting next to them.

We pulled away toward the first tee, and Lucas already let Henry hold onto the wheel and steer.

"Whee," Henry squealed as I prayed we'd make it through the morning.

I had a meeting back at the office in the afternoon, and Henry's nanny was going to spend the rest of the day with him, but Lucas had convinced me that we could talk about the Fall Festival at the orchard on the course. Hence, me riding around with my son in tow on a Wednesday morning instead of being in the office.

We pulled up to the first tee as a group of golfers finished up, which bought us a little time.

"The festival is running for three weekends starting on September twenty-ninth. The petting zoo is already confirmed, along with the pony rides."

I smiled at my cousin, surprised at his sudden interest in this festival. "That's great. Henry is going to love riding the ponies."

Henry nodded and handed me the sucker back for safekeeping.

"Nina sent all the graphics over yesterday, and I think she's already placed the ads for the August and September issues of *Island Times*." I slid out of the golf cart and stretched toward the bright blue sky. "I've paid the deposit on all the food trucks and ordered the bouncy houses. I just need to get with our guy over at the warehouse to see how we can demonstrate how we make the fresh apple juice."

"Awesome." Lucas nodded. "I almost think my

parents charged us with this just to see if we could pull it off."

I laughed and shook my head. "Considering our forties are the next big decade for us, I'd like to believe they have more faith in us than that."

Henry giggled and climbed out of the cart.

"They might have more faith in you than me," Lucas confided as if that were a shock.

The group of golfers in front had long since disappeared, and Lucas pulled out a driver to tee off with.

"What do you think about offering up a little area where some of the town shops can display items to sell?" I asked my cousin.

"You mean like Baubles and Curiosities?" Lucas laughed. "Yeah, I'm sure your girlfriend would love that."

I eyed my cousin, and he shook his head. "Oh, right. Lady friend."

Henry frowned. "What's lady friend?"

"A friend who's a girl."

"Like Meelyah," Henry said. "I like her."

"Me too," I said softly as Lucas took the first swing of the day.

But it also made me realize just how careful I had to be about everything. She'd already left by the time Henry woke up on Monday morning, but I definitely needed to be more careful.

"Nice shot," I called out to Lucas as the bright orange ball rolled into some rough.

Lucas gave me a dirty look, and I got Henry all set up on his tee.

Henry took a couple of swings, missing the ball each time.

"You can throw the ball if you want," I told him.

He threw it with a quick wrist and the ball rolled slowly down the hill.

"Okay, go stand with Lucas. It's Dad's turn."

Henry wandered over to my cousin, and I set up my shot. With a swift and smooth swing, my ball flew straight down the fairway.

"That's how it's done," I told Lucas, who raised his hand at me but thought better of doing any sort of one-finger salute around Henry.

"How's your butt doing?" Lucas asked with a wry grin.

"Completely fine," I assured him. "A few days on the meds, and it feels completely fine."

"What a way to meet the parents," Lucas teased.

"There are so many things I could point out right now, but I'm keeping them to myself." I grinned at Lucas as we climbed back into the golf cart and putted toward our balls. Lucas slowed, and I hopped out to retrieve Henry's ball so it could be closer to ours when we tried again.

As Lucas slowed the cart near his ball in the rough, I thought about Amelia. We'd texted last night, and she said she was working at the store today, but thankfully, she didn't have to watch Oscar any longer since her brother came back from his trip.

But having her be on a completely different island from me was tough. Granted, it only involved a ferry ride and some good planning, but I liked the idea of just being able to see her when I wanted. I thought about this island, which had been home to me for years. My grandpa had expanded the juice headquarters over on this island, and then when the alcohol division took off, we expanded even more.

There just wasn't quite this space on the other island.

But I suppose I didn't always have to be on-site. I had a good team. They knew what to do.

Lucas turned around and shook his head. "Did you see that gust of wind swipe at my ball?"

I laughed. "Is that what they're calling it nowadays?"

"Dude, it was the wind. Right, Henry?"

Henry shrugged, and I chuckled as Lucas climbed back in the golf cart and took off closer to my ball.

"Look at that, would you? Right smack in the middle there?" I pointed at my ball and laughed. "Did you want to hit your ball?"

Henry nodded and climbed out as I handed him his ball and picked out an iron for him. We walked over to my ball, and he put his next to mine and swiped at it.

His club connected with my ball and sent it sailing surprisingly far for a three-year-old.

"That counts," Lucas said from the sidelines. "That totally counts."

"Anything to add an extra swing to my tally." I reached for my phone and took a selfie of Henry and me with our clubs and his grinning face.

"You did awesome," I told him as I picked up the spare ball. At this point, Henry could smack whatever ball he wanted.

"Gonna send that to Amelia?" Lucas asked.

"Send what?"

"The pic."

I shrugged. The thought had crossed my mind.

"Do you think your parents or Nina would care if I spent a bit more time at our grandparents' place?"

Lucas' brows knitted together as he drove us along the path. "No. They'd probably be thrilled about it. They hate how that place just sits there unused."

"Cool." I nodded and hugged Henry close.

"Does this have anything to do with a fascinating antique store you plan on shopping at more often and the ferry ride is just too bothersome?"

"Possibly." I turned to Henry. "Would you like it if we spent more time at the orchard?"

Henry's eyes lit up, and he nodded.

"Good."

Henry's nanny had family on the island, so maybe she wouldn't mind working there too. I'd have to remember to ask her.

When Lucas wasn't looking, I sent the photo of Henry and me to Amelia. Within seconds, she wrote back.

Such a handsome fella

I smiled and shook my head.

Lucas laughed. "I'd know that grin anywhere."

He pulled up to our balls, and we all got off the cart. Lucas went to his since it was farthest away and sliced into the air.

I followed behind and Henry just hung onto his ball.

"The one thing I don't know is how many staff we're

going to need to hire," Lucas said, realizing I wasn't going to elaborate.

"Yeah. If I remember correctly, our grandparents opened it up to the high school kids around the island." I nodded. "I can reach out to the Chamber of Commerce and find out."

"Cool." Lucas lifted Henry back onto the golf cart, and we rode down the pathway.

But all I could think about was spending the rest of the summer at the orchard with Henry and hoping that I'd get to see more of Amelia.

I knew I couldn't make any promises to myself about where things could go with Amelia, but it was fun imagining the possibilities for now.

CHAPTER NINETEEN

Amelia

I lifted the toy milk truck from the 1950s off the shelf and decided it would be perfect for Henry. There was something so cute about it, and the truck would fit in his small hands.

Now, if I were being perfectly honest with myself, I also noticed there was a similar playfulness between the energy of the milk truck and little Henry. I imagined whoever got this toy brand-new so many years ago loved it to death and played with it until the wheels nearly fell off. But I wasn't being honest with myself and just wanted Henry to have a cute toy. I didn't need to get in the habit of making everything as mystical and mysterious as my mom did.

"Did you spot the moving truck over at the orchard?"

Brad asked. He'd just finished up with a customer and wandered over to where I was standing near all the parasols and walking sticks.

"No, I don't drive that way."

"Well, the truck was enormous."

That was odd. James hadn't mentioned anything about moving things in or out.

He'd texted a cute picture of them on the golf course a couple of days ago, but we hadn't really texted much since.

"You've been in it, right?" he asked.

I nodded. "Yeah. Last Sunday."

"And?"

"It was beautiful and stately and very…"

"Very…"

"Regal," I finished.

Dottie waddled over to me and plopped at my feet with a snort.

"Really?"

"It kind of reminded me of a time capsule." I shrugged. "Maybe they're selling some of the stuff. There were antiques everywhere I looked."

Brad laughed and nodded. "Did that make you itchy all over, or did you leave well enough alone?"

"I'm not that bad. It's not like I'm addicted to

antiques."

"Whatever you say."

"I just have an affinity for things that have character."

He rubbed his chin with his thumb and index finger and winked. "Then you must love your brother."

I chuckled and nodded. "You're definitely a character."

The bell from the front door chimed, and I glanced over, trying to see who came inside. I didn't see anyone, so I turned my attention back to my brother.

"Oscar has issues," I told him.

"I know that."

"I mean serious issues."

Brad scowled. "He's just misunderstood."

"No. He's not misunderstood. He's maniacal on his best day, and I don't even want to comprehend what he is on his worst. He bit my date in the ass, and that was after he'd already bit his thumb, not to mention what he'd done to me." I glanced at Dottie. "And let's not forget what he almost did to Dottie."

Brad smirked. "But just imagine the story you can tell your kids about your first date together."

I rolled my eyes as my mom wandered over with a huge grin on her face. "Amelia, you have a customer with a really cute little boy."

My insides tightened at this unexpected Friday surprise, and I held the truck tightly as I wandered to where James and Henry stood with Dottie right behind me.

"Hey, there," I said, glancing at Henry, who had an ice cream cone in his hands. No ice cream, just the cone.

"Wus that?" Henry pointed at the milk truck I had.

"This is for you," I said, bending over to hand it to him.

"Wow." He took the truck from me and giggled, falling to his bum to play in the middle of the store.

James bent down and patted Henry's head. "Say thank you."

"Tanks." Henry beamed, pushing the milk truck on the floor. His thank you was way cuter than I expected.

I looked over to see James studying me, and I smiled. "It reminded me of him. The toy had good energy."

He lifted his brows. "Good energy?"

"Long story." I laughed. "What brought you to this island on this magnificent start to a sunny weekend?"

"I actually have some news I wanted to tell you in person."

Oh, no. They decided to abandon the festival and sell the old estate.

"What's that?" I asked, leaning against the counter full of costume jewelry.

"Henry and I will be hanging out at the orchard most of the summer."

"Wait. What?" I couldn't hide my surprise. "Here?"

James' gaze steadied on mine. "Yeah. It just seems easier with all the planning for the festival and everything."

I smiled. "Oh, yeah? Is that the only reason?"

His right brow arched into an adorable look. "Should there be another?"

Chuckling, I shrugged. "I don't know. Maybe you want to be closer to Oscar."

"Oh, don't mention that cat." He snickered. "He's got some issues."

"Hey, speaking of…" I straightened and glanced at a few customers who came into the building. "What about holding a contest on the last weekend of the festival?"

"What kind of contest? Like an apple pie contest?"

"That sounds like one I'd love to be a judge for, but no." I reached down to Dottie and picked her up. "I was thinking the winner could be an island mascot."

"Why not? Sounds fun."

I nodded in agreement and set Dottie back down.

"What sounds fun?" Brad asked, wandering over.

"I'm not telling you," I joked.

"That's not fair."

"Your sister came up with an island mascot contest for the pets here." James smiled at my brother.

"Oh, I'll have to tell Oscar."

I waggled my index finger in his face. "You'd better not bring that crazy feline. He'll eat the other contestants and make a necklace out of their bones."

Henry giggled, and I realized I'd forgotten he was playing at our feet.

"That's a little extreme, don't you think, Sis?" Brad's eyes widened.

I shrugged. "It's how my mind works."

"Nice to see you again, James." My brother gave a quick nod and wandered toward the back of the store.

I looked up at James and felt all the crazy feelings rushing back. That's all it took now. I could just stand by him and have drunk butterflies crashing into themselves in my stomach.

"Vroom," Henry said, pushing the car along the floor.

I smiled at the miniature version of James and laughed. "I'll be sure to keep an eye out for more cars like that."

James nodded and drew in a breath as his eyes

scanned the store.

"Have you ever taken a look around?" I asked.

He shook his head. "Not really."

"Well, unless you have other plans, how about you wander around while I box up an item for shipping, and then we can hit the café across the way for lunch?"

James' gaze fell to my lips before moving his eyes to mine. "Sounds perfect."

Henry had pushed his car over to a chair full of pillows and turned the other direction. Before I knew it, James swept his lips against mine with a kiss so light, I'd almost missed it.

But it left me wanting more.

So.

Much.

More.

"You're getting as sneaky as Oscar," I teased under my breath.

James laughed. "Except I don't bite."

"That's too bad," I whispered with a glint in my eye.

James teeth ground into his bottom lip as the words settled around him, and he shook his head. "Dang. What are you trying to do to me?"

I chuckled and made my way back to the front counter

to wrap up an item someone bought online.

I'd sneak a look every now and again at James and Henry as they roamed through the antiques. It was always fun to see what items caught people's eyes.

Henry squealed as his tiny hand found a little Alpaca with blue wool. I could tell James was debating whether or not that was a good idea to bring home before he relented.

As I added the last of the packing material, I reached to the tape and secured the box, putting it with the rest for pickup.

When I made it back to the counter, I froze in place as James walked up to the counter with his mother's vase.

The very vase that held the letters and diary.

Did he know?

Did he recognize it?

He set it on the counter next to Henry's Alpaca and glanced in my direction. "Do you think we could just keep these here while we head to lunch? I could see one wrong move eating a sandwich and this thing could break."

I studied the look in his eyes and didn't see any recognition for the piece he chose.

I didn't know whether to point it out or give a big hint or…

Just stay quiet.

I nodded and sucked in a breath as I touched the vase and moved it closer. "Absolutely."

I also didn't feel great about charging him for something that was already his or at least, used to be his.

James leaned over the counter. "Everything okay?"

I let out the big breath I'd sucked in earlier and chewed on my lip for a brief second.

"This…" I stopped myself. "I know I'm going to sound crazy, and I'm okay with that."

James laughed and nodded. "Sure. Crazy can be fun."

I smiled and shook my head. "I've always found it interesting to see what items call out to people when they shop here."

He narrowed his eyes on me. "Are you judging my interior design skills?"

I chuckled and moved my hand from the large vase. "Not at all."

"Then what is it?"

"Often, life has a way of leading us to places and things that somehow touch our heart."

He nodded as Henry petted the Alpaca. "I can see that."

"My mom always believed that our hearts hold all our curiosities. All of the wonderments we've absorbed through the years, our experiences, our likes and dislikes. When our minds don't remember them, our hearts will."

James pulled his brows together and nodded.

"Sometimes, our heart sees and feels things that make absolutely no sense to our mind and yet it's the heart that knows best." I touched the vase and kept my gaze focused on James. "This vase is on the house, and same with the Alpaca."

I couldn't do it. I couldn't tell him.

He shook his head and touched the vase. "No. I insist. You've already given Henry the milk truck. That's plenty. I just liked this vase. It feels...familiar. And unlike my grandparents' house, I don't have much in the way of décor. This ought to add something."

I scratched my head and nodded. "Perfect. But you're not paying for it."

He shifted his gaze to his son and then back to me. "Why's that?"

Oh, phooey!

"Because it's yours."

His hand whipped away from it like it was on fire.

"What do you mean it's mine?"

"That vase came in with the items from your mom's house." I pressed my lips together as my pulse climbed. "It's actually the vase where the letters were hidden and...the diary."

Anger bolted through his gaze, and he took a step back from the vase.

"I'm sorry. I should have told you right when you brought it up. I just wasn't sure how—"

James shook his head and wrapped his hand around Henry's. "I'm assuming that means you got the diary out of it?"

"My brother managed to fish it out. I have it at the house."

"Have you read it?" His voice fell flat.

"Not even a sentence of it," I said softly.

He nodded, still clutching Henry's hand like he was his piece of armor against the vase, against his mom.

"Let's do a raincheck on lunch." James tried to bring a smile to his eyes, but I could feel the rawness of his pain in his words. "Maybe dinner tonight?"

"Are you sure that's enough time?" I asked, feeling my throat tighten.

He'd come into this store so happy with his son, and now he was leaving it completely destroyed.

"Yeah. I just need a little bit of time."

"You didn't recognize it?" I asked.

He shook his head and let out a deep breath. "Tonight

230

at six? Back at the restaurant we never made it to?"

I nodded slowly as I watched James and Henry leave the store, and I realized I felt emptier than I had in a long time.

CHAPTER TWENTY

James

Every bone in my body felt like it shattered along with my heart. The physical pain came at me from out of nowhere.

None of it made sense.

My mom left me when I was a kid. I wasn't of any use to her. She didn't want me. I was nothing more than an item that could be discarded, and that was precisely what she did to me.

And then history repeated itself with my son.

But it had happened decades ago. I'd moved on as much as someone could.

Yet, the exhaustion that slapped itself on me the moment I stared at my mom's vase proved otherwise.

"Are you hungry?" Mary poked her head into the

bedroom of my grandparents' home. "I'm making a grilled cheese and tomato sandwich for Henry. I thought you might like one."

"I'm okay." I nodded. "But thanks for asking."

She walked a few steps into the room. "I know it's not my business, but Henry said something made you sad."

Damn, my boy was perceptive.

Too perceptive.

"Guess there are no secrets in a toddler house." I smiled at Mary.

"Did you break up with that girl you're seeing?" she asked.

"How did you know about her?"

"Well, you suddenly decided to spend the summer at a place you spent your time avoiding, where the woman coincidentally happens to live. And whether you know it or not, you're quite the catch around these islands. Word travels fast when you might be off the market." She chuckled softly. "But I was hoping to spend the summer here too."

"No. I'm still seeing Amelia. It's just…" I let out a deep breath. "Her family's store happens to be the place where all the items from my mom's estate were sent. I was roaming the aisles and found a vase I thought it would be nice to have."

"And it belonged to your mom?"

I nodded. "I have no memory of it whatsoever."

"You might not think you do, but something inside of you knew that it belonged to you."

I nodded slowly. "Yeah. Amelia says it's our heart that collects these connections or curiosities or whatever she said."

"I've always believed that our hearts never lose the spirit of inquiry. It's what pushes love's boundaries and defines happiness. But I'm just some silly old gal, so take it at its worth."

I nodded and smiled.

"Duty calls. I'd better get making that sandwich before Henry thinks I forgot."

"Thanks again for watching him tonight."

"Your date is still on?"

I laughed. "Yeah. I'll pull out of my self-pity mode any second."

When she left the room, I wandered over to my pile of suitcases and opened the small one to display the stack of letters that Amelia handed me.

My Dear Little JJ,

My star baseball player, talented artist, and best

speller in the state, your dreams will always be my dreams. I love you more than you could ever imagine, and I can't wait to watch you grow up to be an incredible and absolutely lovely man. But right now, you're my little JJ, and I'm cherishing all the snuggles we have together.

> *With all my love,*
> *Mommy*

My throat tightened at her words as my finger traced the sentences before I set it down and opened another one.

My Dear Little JJ.

I want you to always know how much you mean to me. Your smile brightens this sometimes-dreary world we live in. It provides hope and shines the light for where love is needed. I'll forever cherish the cuddles we share. My only hope is that you uncover this same kind of love someday.

> *Forever your mommy*

My hand shook as I slid the letter on top of the other. None of this made sense.

None of it.

How could someone pretend to love like that, only to throw it all away?

I opened the third letter.

My Dear Little JJ

You're turning into such a fine little man now. I see the way you hold your head up high on the baseball field. I see how you help the other players find their way. I see YOU, and you make me the proudest mommy alive. I've done things in my past that I'm ashamed of, but having you is what keeps me going. It makes me feel like I have a purpose, that I'm not defined by my mistakes.

And that is something I want you to know when you're older. Don't let your mistakes define you like I've let mine shape me. You can make this world a better place, even if you make a few bad choices along the way.

All my love forever,
Mommy

I walked over to the bedroom door and closed it, making sure to lock it before I slid to the floor, feeling the sharp pains radiate through my entire body with a force that paralyzed me. I'd become the man I was in spite of my mother.

A mother who claimed to love me in these letters but chose to show me otherwise.

I gulped back a wave of tears as anger and confusion ripped through me.

This wasn't love.

This was pretend.

These letters probably made her able to sleep at night.

I reached for another one and opened it up as if it would give me some impossible answer to an impossible question.

Why did you abandon your son?

Dear Little JJ,

Your father would be so proud. I can just see his smile like it was yesterday when you were born. I can feel it now too. I'll always be cheering you on every step of the way. Even if I'm in the shadows, know I'm there.

You might encounter challenges as you grow, but know that nothing is too hard to overcome. The world is a curious place, and your heart will always guide you where

you need to go. Always listen to your heart, Little JJ. It will
make more sense than your mind, especially in trying times.

With all my love,
Mommy

The guttural sound that erupted around me didn't sound human as I pulled a comforter over to muffle my angered cries. I knew I never should have read those letters.

They were just one more complicated lie to add to the incomplete puzzle of my childhood. When I stopped thrashing and took deep breaths to calm my racing pulse, I shoved all the letters back into my suitcase and zipped it up.

Amelia believed that our hearts were full of some sort of mystical inquisitiveness that pulled us to what we needed to experience.

But I would bet a lot of money that I didn't need to experience one word of those letters from the woman who wanted to pretend to care.

Henry's giggles echoed through the air, and I shook my head. No good person would abandon their son like she did to me. I would never do it to my son. I would never do it like Masha did to Henry.

My jaw clenched as I thought about my ex. I'd been careful to not let her name even enter my brain since she handed Henry over and said she couldn't do it.

Couldn't do what?

Be decent?

Was that too much to ask?

Could she not just at least show up on his birthdays?

I shook my head and pushed myself off the floor and went to the window overlooking the water. Why did Masha and my mom not understand that abandoning their sons did more damage than good?

I was a grown man, and I still had abandonment issues. Issues that weren't going away. They were only getting worse.

There wasn't a day that went by where I wondered when Amelia was going to get tired of me. When she'd come to her senses and realize I was truly screwed up. The only good thing I really understood about myself was being Henry's father. It was an honor to raise him, and I couldn't understand anyone who thought otherwise. My only hope was to smother Henry in so much love that he didn't ever stop to ask where his mom was or why she never came to visit.

I wiped my palms over my face and groaned at the wreck of myself I'd managed to hide from the world.

The pain that I pretended didn't exist always nipped at the surface, but it was Henry who took it away.

And now Amelia.

I smiled faintly as I stood, leaning on the glass and wondering what I truly wanted.

Was it even possible?

I walked to the bathroom and turned on the shower to get ready for the date. Hopefully, I wouldn't show up looking as shitty as I felt.

No woman needed to see a guy show up for a date with mommy issues and puffy eyes.

As the steam rolled into the room, I stripped off my clothes and climbed under the hot water. The beads rolled down my skin as I thought about Amelia.

The way her lips would pucker right before she was about to laugh. How she laughed all the time, even when she probably shouldn't.

And her green eyes.

I loved her green eyes and how her gaze always felt like she was holding back a little secret. I wanted to know what that secret was. I wanted to know everything about Amelia.

I needed to know everything about her.

Just the thought started to make me feel better. The

thought of Amelia made my world feel right and like I could handle anything.

Letting out a deep groan as I washed the soap off my skin, I knew what I needed to do tonight. It was the only way I'd get any sort of closure.

CHAPTER TWENTY-ONE

Amelia

Dottie sat at my feet and whined while I finished up with a customer at the store. I felt as unsettled as she did, but at least I knew what would fix her.

As the customers left, I bent down and put her leash on to take her outside. The moment I stepped onto the sidewalk, the warm July weather kissed my skin and the sweet smell of roses drifted through the air.

I walked Dottie down the sidewalk to the park across the block. She hadn't been out much today since the store was so busy, and I was happy for the break.

Ever since James scurried out of the store with Henry, my stomach was in knots and my chest felt tight with worry.

I didn't even know what I was worried about most.

Was James upset at me about the vase? Did he realize I was a little too into my antiques and the value they held to some?

Dottie let out a couple of quick yelps of excitement, and I glanced over to see Bryce walking Herman this way.

"Hello there, stranger," Bryce said with a grin.

Herman pranced over to Dottie and sniffed her in a way that made Dottie blush. She sat down and stared at me in frustration.

"Would you control your dog?" I rolled my eyes, and Bryce laughed.

"There's nothing I can do about how Herman feels about Dottie. Sometimes, you just have to let these things play out. Maybe we've got a little enemies-to-lovers going on here." He wiggled his brows.

"In his dreams."

"I don't doubt it."

"Is it true that James Edwards is moving back to this island? I saw the moving trucks, and someone at Maddie's tea shop was talking about it this morning."

"Just for the summer," I explained. "But who knows? That could have changed since this morning."

He frowned. "Why's that?"

"Long story."

"I've got time. I'm self-employed."

"Shouldn't that make you work harder?"

"Not when there's a juicy story in the making."

"I don't understand how you're more of a gossip than anyone in my parents' bridge club."

"I'm not a gossip. I just listen to pieces of information that are disseminated in my direction and carefully construct an interesting narrative that is seldom in the vicinity of being correct."

I chuckled. "At least you recognize it."

"So, spill the beans."

"There's not much to spill."

"Does it have to do with his mom?"

My gaze flashed back to his. "How do you know about his mom?"

He shrugged. "Just a hunch."

I narrowed my eyes on him.

"Fine. My aunt and his mom ran in the same crowd when they were younger, and by all accounts from my mom, it wasn't a good crowd."

"Whatever that means." I shrugged, but my interest was definitely piqued.

"It was why I lived with my grandparents for a couple of years."

Herman lay down, and Dottie curled up to him, and I

scowled. "Maybe you're onto something about these dogs. If this is any indication about how love is supposed to work, I'm doomed."

Bryce looked shocked. "Wait a second. What is going on? When have you ever cared about falling in love? Are you in love with James? Is that why he's moving here?"

"Just for the summer," I chimed in. "But no, I'm not in love. It's all very complicated, and he might decide not to stay anyway after today."

"Does any of this have to do with what you tried to give him?"

"Maybe. I don't know. I just tried to explain to him how the items in our store often pick the people instead of the people picking the items."

I really didn't feel like droning on about how there were no coincidences in life, and James had been handed a real raw deal in his childhood that he kept sweeping under the rug, but there was a chance that we might actually be a good fit. But not until he dealt with his stuff and I dealt with mine.

But the odds weren't exactly in our favor.

"Listen, I know you better than you'd ever want to admit, but sometimes, you overthink things. You want to paint things with a magical brush that explains away behavior and promises actions that can't actually happen in the real world."

"Tell me how you really feel."

He smiled. "I just did. There isn't always some mystical explanation for why someone buys an old, embroidered pillow in your store. Maybe the person just liked the colors. But if you go trying to heal some deep family wounds blabbering about souls touching and the stars aligning, it might not end up like you want."

I pressed my lips together into a thin line and bent over to give Dottie some extra ear scratches while I pushed away my embarrassment. Was this how Bryce and everyone else saw me? A laughingstock? Was this why my fiancé dumped me and ran off with my best friend? Because I believed too much in happenstance?

He squeezed my shoulder. "I'm not saying you're not right, Mel. I tend to think that things happen for a reason too."

I hated when he called me that, and if my expression didn't tell him that now, it never would.

"But maybe he just wants to be heard instead of lectured to about things." He let go of my shoulder and I let out a deep breath.

Bryce was right.

Maybe it was just time to listen and hope he wanted to be heard. Not every problem was meant to be solved.

"Will you still talk to me after this?" he teased,

pulling on Herman's leash.

I smiled. "Probably."

"Tell me how everything goes," he said, turning around with Herman as Dottie looked forlorn.

"Don't tell me you have a crush on the toothless wonder?" I whispered.

Dottie glanced up at me and her tongue fell out of her mouth.

"Great," I muttered, walking Dottie back to the store.

"I wondered if you'd ran away with my Dottie," my mom said, eyeing us as we came inside.

I unhooked Dottie's leash, and she wandered over to my mom and sat down.

"No. I ran into Bryce and you know how that goes."

My mom chuckled. "He's a talker."

"But this time, he might have had some valid points."

"About what?"

"Men, I guess."

She didn't look convinced. "Speaking of, I'm headed out to meet James in a few minutes. It's Mae's turn to close tonight."

A wry smile spread across my mom's mouth. "Well, enjoy your date. I heard he decided to spend the summer on the island."

"Yeah, I think the entire island has already heard that."

"That will be good."

I raised my shoulders. "Hopefully."

"You've never been pessimistic. Don't start now."

I laughed to myself as I walked out of the store. That was one thing my fiancé didn't like about me. Well, there were apparently many things. But he often felt like I was too cheery.

Not that it mattered. I'd healed those wounds.

I was sure of it.

Besides, it was a lovely July evening to have a walk, and I was about to have an amazing dinner with someone I couldn't get enough of.

It was hard to believe that it was July, but the warm temperatures made it clear.

By the time I got inside the restaurant, I was hot and thirsty.

I didn't even bother to wait for James and just asked the hostess to seat me so I could get something to drink.

The server filled up our water glasses just as I saw James arrive in a black T-shirt that read *I Heart Cats*.

James followed the hostess to our table, and it was nearly impossible to rip my gaze away. His incredibly broad shoulders stretched the fabric across his chest, and his massive biceps snuck out of the short sleeves.

I realized I was licking my lips and quickly smacked my lips shut when he arrived.

"I'm sorry for sitting. I was so thirsty by the time I got here, but I think that's really because I was standing in the heat with Dottie talking to Bryce at the park before I made my way over here."

He laughed and sat down, taking the menu from the hostess. "No problem. I would have done the same."

James looked much less like he'd seen a ghost and far calmer now that he was sitting here with me rather than in the antique store. I wasn't sure I should bring up the vase, so I took a sip of water and scanned the menu.

"I love Italian. Thanks for bringing me to me Cardelli's." I peeked over the menu at James and realized he'd been studying me with a smile. "I think I'm going to have the manicotti."

I shut the menu, and his smile only grew. "Are you always this incredible?"

Glancing around the restaurant, I leaned in and laughed. "Is the manicotti your favorite too?"

James laughed and sat back in the seat and closed the menu. "It's pretty good. I'm not gonna lie, but I think tonight

I'll have the chicken parmigiana."

I nodded in agreement as he slowly cupped his hands together.

"So, about earlier at the store," he said, and I quickly shook my head.

But then Bryce's comment from earlier popped into my head, and I decided to keep my lips sealed and let James talk.

"I want to apologize for leaving abruptly and not taking the vase with me."

"That's okay."

The server took our order and left while James kept his gaze on me. "It's not okay, at least not without some explanation. You don't need a guy who suddenly vanishes anytime a reminder from his past pops up."

I brought in a slow breath and glanced out the window to see a family wandering down a pier toward their boat. Should I mention that I specialized in men who vanished?

"I'm a grown man who shouldn't be stuck in the past. I have an amazing little boy, a great business, and the ability to make my own schedule when and where I want it."

I nodded in agreement, but I still didn't want to say anything.

"But I'm far more…" He stopped himself and glanced

out the window. "I think the technical term is screwed up…
than I ever want to admit."

A muscle in his jaw twitched as he shook his head and
took a sip of water.

"I want to be there for you," I said softly. "Society
always makes us feel like we have to go at things alone and
that we have to fix our issues independently, but it's easier
with help. It's the kinder way to do it."

James' expression softened, and he nodded. "I don't
want my little boy seeing me freeze and have an internal
meltdown over a vase or over anything. I just…"

"You just," I prompted.

"I just have kept things in for so long that I don't even
know how to talk about them. Even today, I went home and
screamed into a comforter."

I smiled and nodded. "That's a start."

"I've spent my entire life pretending I didn't have a
mother. I worked hard to push out all my earlier memories of
her so the core memory of her leaving would hurt less. But it
didn't work. I'll be forty in a couple of years, and I still can't
think about my mom without getting ill."

I kept my gaze on him, feeling the raw pain roll off
him with every passing memory flooding his mind.

"I can't imagine feeling abandoned like that." I shook

my head. "Especially not having anywhere to land afterward."

He ran his fingers through his hair. "My grandparents."

"We haven't talked that much about them, but it sounded like to me they weren't exactly warm and fuzzy. It doesn't sound like much of a soft landing."

"No." He nodded in agreement. "I felt like a burden."

His words gutted me. No child should ever feel like a burden.

"But with every passing year, I excelled. I made sure I got the best grades I could get or that if I picked up a sport, I'd excel at it. I always felt like if I could be better or do better, then maybe people wouldn't want to get rid of me."

I gasped at his admission and sat back in awe. My eyes canvased this hulk of a man who held such pain and grief for something over which he had no control.

"That maybe my mom would come back."

I did not pity the man in front of me. I admired him.

He straightened his arms onto the table and twiddled his thumbs as he thought about what next to say, but I couldn't stay quiet any longer.

"You deserve better, and you're ensuring that Henry has better."

James broke into a smile, and he nodded. "Thank you.

I just don't understand how I managed to pick a woman who was like my mom and wanted nothing to do with raising a child."

I nodded, unsure of what to say to that. I knew nothing about his ex.

"I read the letters from my mom," he said quietly.

My brows rose in surprise. "All of them?"

He ran a napkin through his fingers. "All of them. I read a few before I took a shower and then decided to read the rest."

"Are you okay?"

James laughed and shook his head. "Not really. No, but I hope to get there."

The letter I read felt so full of love that I couldn't fathom how that same woman could just stop seeing her son.

"And I think I'd like that diary you said you had."

"Absolutely."

"And the vase."

I nodded and took a deep breath as I looked into James' eyes and for the first time ever, saw a bit of hope.

CHAPTER TWENTY-TWO

James

My heart raced as I looked into Amelia's eyes. The soft glow of the moonlight cast an intoxicating glow around her that pulled me closer. We stood by her front door as a gentle breeze rustled the leaves and carried the scent of lavender our way, but all I could think about was kissing her.

She looked up into my eyes and smiled that cute little pouty grin I couldn't get enough of. There was no denying the electricity in the air that acted like a magnetic force, drawing us closer.

Even things that should scare her away didn't.

I was a single dad.

I had issues.

So many issues.

I cleared my throat. "Did you want me to wait here while you go get the diary?"

Amelia looped her finger around the collar of my T-shirt and smiled coyly.

"Why don't you come in?" she asked softly.

"Are you sure?"

"I have zero doubts." She pulled me inside and gently kicked the door closed behind me.

I noticed the flowers I'd sent her when we first met were upside down, hang-drying by the window.

"What are you going to do with me, James?" she asked breathlessly, moving to close the gap between us.

I smiled at her as my eyes locked on hers, the longing sweeping through her gaze. The dance was intoxicating.

The room filled with charges of electricity as she moved her hand along my back, driving my need for her to new heights.

"I don't know what I can promise," I whispered. "I want you to know that."

She nodded and looked at me through her thick lashes. "I understand."

"We have to take things slow."

"Slow," she breathed as her fingers worked the hem of my T-shirt over my head. She pressed her soft lips to my bare chest, and I thought I was going to lose it that second.

I desperately wanted to kiss her.

"No promises," she whispered as she silently begged for a kiss. "I understand."

But the truth was that I wanted to promise her the world. I wanted to be the man who could be everything for her and more.

I didn't want to be the guy who was haunted by his past and couldn't carve out a great future.

But I couldn't promise I wasn't him.

She licked her lips slowly, and my body lit on fire with raw need for Amelia.

I moved my mouth to hers, cradling the back of her head in my hands as I brought her forward. My tongue pushed through her lips, and she kissed me back.

Amelia's kiss was eager and demanding as I tasted the sweetness of her lips. Her hands ran along my bare skin, and I quickly worked to take her shirt off. When I tossed it to the floor, I took a step back and memorized her beautiful curves as she flushed and giggled while taking off her own bra. She dangled the pink lace in front of me and whipped it to the side, and I couldn't help but smile.

The fullness between her breasts and her hips made me so hard it physically hurt. She moved toward me, and I kissed her again.

She nipped my bottom lip as her breathing increased while I moved my hands under the waistband of her pants until my fingers touched the lace of her underwear.

I worked my fingers lower as her breath hitched between kisses.

"Don't stop," she whispered as I moved my thumb in between her folds and her body pressed into mine.

Her hands worked the button of my pants undone as she moved my briefs aside and gripped me tight.

I hissed from her touch as our hands worked in a perfect rhythm. When I felt her body tighten, I kissed her harder and slowed my movements, careful not to let her fall over the edge.

Her grip lessened slightly as I kicked my pants off my ankles before scooping her into my arms and taking her to bed.

"A studio can come in handy," she teased as her eyes stayed on mine. They were wild with the same need I felt.

I set her down below me and moved my mouth along her stomach. Her body quivered as my touch went lower along with my lips.

Her hips wriggled for more as I moved my mouth away and stayed on top of her, penning her in with my elbows.

"I want to feel you," she said softly, looking into my

eyes. "All of you."

I smiled and nodded, nudging her knees wider as I found her warmth and moved my lips to hers, teasing her and tasting her.

Her fingers moved through my hair as I drove into her, feeling her clench around me. Her kisses became rawer and more ragged with every thrust. She wrapped her legs around me, grinding her hips into me as I moved my mouth down to her breasts, playing and tugging on each nipple.

"You feel so good," she breathed, curling her head into the nook of my shoulder.

She let out a little hum, and my body ignited. Our bodies brushed against one another, and the tension raised as our whispers of need grew every second.

I felt her clench around me as her breathing quickened and her nails dug into my back.

It felt so good.

The release of every emotion I'd bottled became an intoxicating force as we surrendered to the realness of the moment. Nothing else mattered but having her in my arms. We could work everything out.

Somehow.

It would work between us.

It had to.

Time stood still as we lost ourselves again, and there was no denying that our bodies moved in perfect harmony. I couldn't get enough of her.

Amelia snuggled into my chest, her bare body against mine as I held her close. I'd never felt this intimacy with another person. There was something going on between us that I couldn't understand, but I was so afraid it would disappear.

As if sensing my thoughts, she looked up at me and smiled.

"I think that I've really been missing out all these years," she said, knitting her brows together in the cutest expression of bewilderment and euphoria.

"Is that so?"

"Definitely so." She shook her head and pulled up the sheet. "I was completely unaware that sex could be so mind-blowing."

I laughed, pulling her closer. "Well, I'm glad I could be the one to enlighten you."

"Can you enlighten me again and again?"

CHAPTER TWENTY-THREE

Amelia

I glanced over at the last stack of boxes in the container from the Edwards estate. No box ever disappointed, but it made me feel odd for making far more profit than he ever had on these things.

But I knew how he felt about the person who owned them, and he seemed to think this was the healthiest way to deal with things.

I wasn't so sure.

The sun cast a warm glow into the storage container, giving me just enough light to see the few remaining boxes.

Brad appeared just in time, and I gave him an evil grin. "Do you mind pulling that box down so I can go through it?"

"Sure thing." He reached for the cardboard box effortlessly and slid it in front of me.

"So, have things between you and James gotten serious?" he asked, taking a sip of soda and setting it on the ground.

I fidgeted with the hem of my T-shirt as I looked over at my older brother. His arms were crossed over his chest, and his brows were furrowed in that familiar concerned expression that had been etched into his features since we were kids. He leaned against the opening to the storage container and waited for my reply.

"Uh, maybe." I couldn't hide my smile. "Yes."

Brad pushed himself off the doorframe and took a tentative step into the container, which suddenly made it feel even stuffier. This wasn't exactly what I wanted to reveal to my brother, of all people.

I took a deep breath, bracing myself for his reaction.

He nodded, his expression softening slightly. "You know I'm always here to listen, right? You can talk to me about anything."

I nervously gnawed on my lower lip. "It's getting pretty serious, Brad. And I know you're probably going to worry, but I just wanted to talk to you about it."

Brad kneeled next to me, and his eyes locked onto mine.

I managed a small smile. "I think this could actually go somewhere."

He reached out and gave my shoulder a reassuring squeeze. "Okay, spill it. What has you worried?"

I took another deep breath. "Remember what happened with my last relationship?"

His face grew serious, his jaw tensing. "I don't think any of us could forget that. It probably scared the rest of us away from settling down too."

"I hope not, but I'm kind of worried it did that to me," I admitted, my voice barely above a whisper. "And that's why I'm so scared, Brad. I've been hurt before, and I don't want to go through that again. But James seems so different, and he's been through so much. He genuinely cares about me. I can feel it."

"But?" Brad's gaze remained fixed on me, his expression thoughtful.

"But I think we both wonder who will run away first."

Brad grimaced and shook his head. "I want you to be happy, Sis. You deserve someone who treats you well and makes you happy, but you also have to take ownership. You can't let fear dictate your actions. Hopefully, he won't either."

Tears welled, and I shook my head, embarrassed. "Between you and Bryce, I'm starting to realize that you actually do have emotions."

He leaned in and hugged me. "I just want you to know that I'm here for you, no matter what. If he makes you happy and treats you right, then I'll support your decision. But don't run. Let it play out."

I nestled into the hug, taking in his brotherly love. "You have no idea how much this means to me."

He pulled away slightly and looked into my eyes. A sloppy grin tugged at the corner of his lips. "Just promise me one thing, okay?"

I nodded, my heart pounding with anticipation. "Anything."

"Promise me that you'll always value yourself. Don't let someone tell you that you're not worth anything. You're the most amazing woman, and you've managed to hold your head up high through all kinds of things beyond a broken relationship."

"Two broken relationships," I said softly, thinking back to my ex-BFF.

"Exactly. Just no matter what happens between you and James, don't ever let him or anyone make you feel less than you are."

Tears spilled down my cheeks as a mixture of gratitude flooded over me. "As long as you or my sisters don't run off with him, I should be just fine."

Brad laughed and shook his head. He wiped my tears with his thumb and gave me a gentle smile. "I'm not into facial hair, hairy legs, things like that…"

"Believe me. I know. The moment you turned thirteen, you covered your room in posters that I still can't get out of my head. I didn't know they made swimsuits that small."

As I looked into my brother's eyes, I saw not only my overprotective brother, but I also saw someone who genuinely cared about my well-being more than his own.

Not all men were dogs, no offense to the canine community.

And I hoped Brad could find his happily-ever-after too.

"Okay, I'd better get back at it." I stretched my hands toward the container's ceiling and pretended to crack my knuckles. "I'm headed over to the orchard for dinner."

Brad's smile only widened. "I can't tell you how happy that makes me."

"Oh, speaking of…I just found out a place down the road is coming up for rent. Would you come look at it with me next week?"

He nodded. "Absolutely."

I gave him a wave and bent over the box to cut the tape off the top.

When the cardboard flaps sprang open, it felt like all the air in the storage container had been sucked out when I looked inside. The box was full of toys and memorabilia from James' childhood. It had to be his. My chest tightened with the realization that he didn't even know that his mom kept all these things for all these years. The ache in my body grew as I tried my hardest to understand what could have possibly gone on to have him feel so abandoned or why she felt she could no longer raise him.

The air was thick with melancholy as I stared at these treasures. I could almost hear the echoes of a little boy's laughter as my hands clutched a teddy bear on top that had a tattered green ribbon and a torn ear.

This was what happened to be with found objects. Their stories would sweep me away into another time and place, but I never expected it to happen today.

Not with James' own history.

My throat constricted as I stared at the jumble of items in this box. They definitely belonged to James. I reached for the faded baseball cap with the logo of his Little League team and shook my head in disbelief. He had no idea that these items were even around.

I held the cap in my hands, imagining James wearing it proudly as his mom cheered on the sidelines. It was like a movie churning through me. Everything I pictured was so vivid and alive. I found a yo-yo and held it close, feeling more emotion rush through me as I imagined James showing off yo-yo tricks for his mom. I pushed some items aside and saw an old video game console and laughed.

I shook my head, realizing that for some reason, I'd never pictured James as an ordinary kid who'd play video games. It was like once he told me he'd been shipped off to boarding school, I came up with my own version of him. Now, I could picture him sitting in front of the TV, his eyes wide with excitement as he played the games.

As I rummaged through the box, my fingers brushed against a small collection of action figures. I held up a worn-out superhero with the paint chipped off its shoulders. I couldn't help but smile at the thought of my boyfriend dealing blows in epic battles and lost in his own imagination, his own innocence.

And then, instantly, it was all stripped away.

A tattered journal caught my eye, and my stomach roiled with anxiety. I opened it slowly and saw its pages filled with James' writing. I started to read it and closed it quickly. It didn't seem right to glimpse into his thoughts from so long ago when I knew how the story ended. In that brief moment, it felt like I peered into his young mind and experienced his dreams taking shape.

I picked up the teddy bear again and wondered if James had turned to this teddy bear during moments of loneliness when he'd been left behind at his grandparents' house?

I came across a stack of drawings neatly tucked at the bottom of the box. I carefully flipped through them. It was hard not to admire the crude yet endearing sketches. Animals with three heads, family members with pink and blue hair, and fantastical creatures covered the papers. It was clear that art had been a way for James to express himself, but I wondered if that ended, too, when he was pulled away from his mother.

But I just couldn't imagine that his mother hadn't loved him.

Didn't love him.

I felt there was so much more to this story, but it wasn't mine to uncover.

Lost in my thoughts, I realized that I had spent hours immersed in my boyfriend's childhood memories and would miss dinner if I didn't leave now.

But there was no denying it. I felt a deeper connection to him now, like there were these little bits of stories woven together to offer a glimpse into his early childhood, but I wanted to know more.

I carefully placed the items back into the box and made a mental note to ask James about each piece, to hear his stories and relive those moments with him. I bet Henry would get a kick out of seeing his dad's old toys too.

With the box in my arms, I made it to my car and shoved it into the backseat and took off to the orchard.

When I pulled up, the gate was already open, and I drove through to see the sprawling mansion. James was out front playing catch with Henry, using a huge bouncy ball that neither of them could keep track of.

I turned off the car and felt the familiar skip in my heart rate when James looked over at me.

Henry ran to the ball and picked it up, grinning at me over the top of the huge rubber ball.

"Meelya," he said happily as James came over and hugged me.

I was surprised since we hadn't really spoken about next steps or about Henry, but I eagerly returned the hug. James brushed a quick kiss over my lips, and it felt like my knees would buckle if he turned away.

"Thanks for inviting me over for dinner," I said as he took a step back and reached for the ball from Henry.

James flashed a wry grin. "Don't get too impressed. I'm only making bratwurst and potato salad."

I laughed and shrugged. "Sounds like my kind of dinner."

Henry toddled over to me and held up his hand. I wrapped mine around his little fingers, and he squeezed back.

He looked up at me and grinned, and I felt like my world was finally complete.

"Will you be my mommy?" Henry asked.

James froze, and his gaze flashed to mine. I saw every emotion pummeling through his expression as I found my words.

But I knew no words would be the right ones.

"Hey, buddy," James said, kneeling down next to him. "Amelia is our very good friend, and we're just loving her company now, right?"

Henry nodded, slipping his hand away from mine.

"We're just taking one step at a time," he explained as Henry cocked his head and glanced at me. "Does that make sense?"

"No."

James nodded. "Okay. Well, it will."

"Let's play tag," Henry hollered, but when James stood up, I could see it in his eyes.

He didn't have to tell me anything.

I just knew.

CHAPTER TWENTY-FOUR

James

I kept replaying the night that changed everything, and I still didn't know how I should have handled it. Why didn't I have a game plan in place? That was so irresponsible of me. The least I could have done with Amelia was go over something.

Anything.

And to do that to Amelia? She didn't deserve what happened. I knew I never should have let myself fall for her.

When she told me there was a box of mine that she thought I might want and Henry might enjoy, she was nearly in tears. I took the box out of her car, and she couldn't drive away fast enough.

She hadn't returned any of my texts since then, and I

didn't blame her.

It had been two weeks.

I sat on the edge of my bed with my hands trembling as I stared at the words that I'd written in a diary so long ago. Page after page about how much my mom loved me or where she took me to play, or how we had to hunt down tickets to a sold-out baseball game.

Things I'd long since forgotten.

Things that showed a love I'd pretended didn't exist.

But I had to forget those things in order to survive. I couldn't let myself dwell on the mountain of loss that didn't let me loose enough to climb free.

I ran my palm over my face and let out a groan of frustration.

I had no idea my mom had saved these things, and all it did was add more confusion to the picture I had painted of this woman. How could she give me up and never see me again or even attempt to see me again, yet keep everything from my childhood?

And Amelia knew. She knew how much I didn't know about my life. I only identified what had been told to me or constructed around me.

It was no wonder that I chose my ex. It was like I'd tried to find the most unavailable woman to have a child with.

And now, the weight of my decision pressed heavily on my chest. I was drowning in a suffocating mix of guilt and sorrow. It felt like a piece of my soul got torn away when Amelia and I broke up. Yet, it was the best thing to do for Henry. I didn't need to start parading different women in front of him, having him get attached, and then they all abandoned him.

He didn't need that kind of life on repeat.

Henry was only a room away, sleeping peacefully down the hallway. Thankfully, he seemed unaware of the turbulence that had consumed me since Amelia drove away.

Henry's innocence was a stark contrast to the turmoil raging within me. Each laugh he threw my way or echo of "I love you" reminded me that I had made the right decision for him.

He needed stability.

It was my duty to provide stability.

I walked out of my bedroom and snuck a peek at Henry. It was three o'clock in the afternoon, and he'd crashed for a nap after playing all morning in the orchard.

Even though I'd moved us here for the rest of the summer to be closer to Amelia, the choice was still a good one. Henry loved it here, and I didn't blame him.

I made my way down the stairs to see Mary sipping

some coffee at the kitchen island.

"I haven't seen Amelia around lately."

The mention of her made my stomach clench. I missed her so much. I missed what the future with her meant.

I shrugged and poured myself a cup of coffee.

"It's complicated."

"Relationships are seldom simple." She nodded and took a sip.

"I messed up. I knew I should have paced it better and not let my emotions get in the way of doing the right thing."

Mary cocked her head slightly. "And what is the right thing?"

"Not getting involved," I explained as if it were obvious.

She frowned. "So, you think it's better to just stay single until Henry is an adult?"

"Pretty much."

"I always do my best to agree with the person who pays me, but that is the most ridiculous thing I've heard."

I choked a laugh out and smiled. "Thanks, Mary. But it's not ridiculous. My son asked her if she would be his mommy?"

"And?"

"What do you mean, and...?" I shoved my fingers

through my hair and shook my head. "That's huge. That's scary," I said flatly.

Mary's brown eyebrows shot up. "For whom? You or Henry?"

I stayed silent.

"Isn't it a good thing that he feels comfortable enough around Amelia to consider the possibility of her sticking around?"

I still didn't say a word.

"You know, Henry asked me if I would be his mom." She eyed me, but I wouldn't let my surprise surface.

"I didn't know that."

"It's only natural," she said softly.

"But I don't want to parade a ton of women around Henry and have him get confused."

Mary folded her arms over her chest. "Then don't."

"It's not fair to him."

"It's not fair to you either," she said softly. "And I don't think we're talking about you parading women in front of him. That's not who you are. You are in love with one woman. One."

I ground my molars together as I thought about what Mary was saying.

"I think the person who is scared is you, James. It's

not Henry. He's three. He'll be fine."

Taking my cup of coffee, I walked over to the windows overlooking the water. Usually, the view would offer me solitude, but my emotions were so raw and all over the place that the sight just made me seasick with emotion.

The doorbell chimed and Mary put her cup of coffee down.

"The gate must be open. Are you expecting anyone?" she asked.

I shook my head and let out a slow breath, wishing for something that wasn't possible.

This wasn't like one of those fairy tales where Amelia would show up, and I'd confess how sorry I was and what a terrible mistake I'd made.

The moment I heard Lucas' voice booming through the house, I was swiftly reminded that this was real life.

I turned around and glanced at him.

He flinched. "Man, you look awful. When was the last time you shaved?"

I rolled my eyes and took a sip of coffee. "It's not that bad."

"Whatever you say." He walked over and let out a yawn.

"Need some coffee?" I asked, holding my cup.

"Yeah. Sounds good."

"Great. You know where the cups are. Help yourself."

Lucas chuckled. "Such service."

"I think I'm going to head out soon," Mary said, glancing over after rinsing her cup out in the sink. "Unless there's something else you need."

"No. Not at all. Thanks for the pep talk, Mary."

She nodded and headed toward the foyer.

Lucas shook his head. "A pep talk?"

After pouring his cup, he wandered to the family room and sat on the floral loveseat. There wasn't a moment that went by that didn't remind me that this was my grandparents' home, no matter how opulent.

Lucas leaned back and sipped his coffee. He studied me intently.

"You've got that look about you," he said, his voice laced with a knowing smile.

I gave him a dirty look. "What look?"

"The one that tells me you're wrestling with something big."

I sighed, tracing the rim of my cup with my finger. "I screwed up, and there's no going back."

A soft grin tugged at the corner of his lips. "There's always a way."

I hesitated, searching for the right words. "I broke up with her."

He raised an eyebrow, genuine surprise coloring his expression. "Wait. Why would you do that?"

I nodded, a knot forming in my throat. "It felt like the right thing to do. Well, I didn't exactly do it...She just knew..."

Lucas leaned forward, his gaze unwavering. "I don't get it. You really liked her. Henry liked her."

I nodded. "He liked her too much. He asked if she'd be his mommy."

Lucas blew out some air and nodded. "That's a big one."

"It is."

"But not something to break up with her over. It's not her fault she's charming and sweet. What three-year-old wouldn't love her?"

I laughed and shook my head, sitting on the couch. Leave it to my cousin.

"Well, I screwed it up. She won't return my calls or texts." I rubbed my brows and groaned. "She made me smile. The only person who's truly made me smile in my life is Henry. And then I met her."

Lucas scowled. "I take offense."

I leaned over and propped my elbow on my knee. "Is that a surprise? I'm starting to realize that since my adult life, I keep repeating mistakes that others have done to me. The first moment of a ripple, and I bolt," I explained. My voice was soft but determined. "I thought that by walking away, I was letting go of the pain, the turmoil, and all the chaos that could come with having a real relationship with Amelia. But I've come to understand that I also let go of something beautiful."

Lucas' eyes softened, a glimmer of understanding shining through. "You're saying you miss her."

"I'm saying she's my future, and I blew it." I nodded, my chest heavy with the confession. "I miss her smile, the way she'd laugh at my terrible jokes, the way her lips move into an adorable pucker." I let out a sigh. "And all of the late-night conversations that stretched until dawn. We'd call and then we'd text and neither of us wanted to stop."

Lucas leaned back and tapped his fingers rhythmically on the coffee table. "So, what are you going to do about it?"

I shrugged. "Just suffer the consequences. She doesn't want anything to do with me."

He swiped his hand in the air. "Nah. So what if she's ignoring your calls and texts. Maybe she's busy? That wouldn't stop me."

"Well, there's this law about stalking people—"

His laughter cut me off. "Come on, dude. Either you're gonna fight for the woman of your dreams or you're going to dream about the woman you lost because you lost your fight."

"I just don't want Henry to get confused."

"Why would he get confused? He set his sights on her, and now it's up to you to make your little boy happy."

My cousin let out a thoughtful sigh. "Regret is a tough emotion to grapple with, but you'll feel even worse if you don't try."

I ran a hand through my hair, exhaling slowly. "You're right."

Lucas reached across the table, placing his hand on mine. "Maybe it's not about rewriting the past. Maybe it's about accepting your past and being willing to create a new future with someone who has the compassion that Amelia has. That would be really powerful for Henry to grow up being surrounded by."

I met his gaze, gratitude welling up within me. "You always know how to put things into perspective, which always surprises the shit out of me."

He chuckled, giving my hand a reassuring squeeze. "I

don't know whether to be flattered or offended."

"Henry should be waking up soon. Do you mind watching after him while I go find Amelia?"

"My pleasure. She shouldn't be hard to find. And remember, no matter what, I've got your back."

CHAPTER TWENTY-FIVE

Amelia

"He warned me plenty of times." I shook my head and took a sip of tea.

Bryce and I were sitting on the teashop's patio overlooking the ferries.

"It's not like he didn't tell me that he couldn't go down that path with me. He did." I nodded as if to reassure myself that it was my fault. "I missed the signs."

Bryce waited until I'd finished and then turned his gaze toward me.

"You did nothing wrong," he said flatly.

"I did everything wrong." I shook my head. "You should have seen the little boy. He was so cute when he said those words to me, and I couldn't even think of anything to say."

Bryce nodded. "Maybe on some level, it's because you wanted it to be true."

"That's just crazy. We've only dated a couple of months."

"You and I both know that you wouldn't have even considered going out with him unless you saw a future." Bryce shook his head. "It's okay to imagine a future, you know. History doesn't have to repeat itself. Maybe it's time to change your narrative. Quit being the woman who lost her best friend to her fiancé. Be the fiancée and lover of old things who becomes a great mom."

"That's a stretch. Besides, he's got a lot of things to work through. He's never recovered from his mom leaving him all those years ago, and to be honest, I'd be the same way."

He nodded slowly and picked up his phone to send a quick text.

Bryce scowled. "Haven't you ever heard about manifesting?"

I shrugged. "And it's worked for you?"

He nodded. "When I've applied it."

"Like when?"

"Herman, for one. I wanted a dog who wouldn't hurt

a soul and who got overlooked in life. In came Herman, a toothless pooch with a heart of gold who just scares people by existing."

"Okay. Why don't you manifest yourself a girlfriend then?"

"I'm too afraid of the results. I'm telling you, it really works, and I'm not sure I know what I want yet. What if I manifest a nightmare?"

"Well, you certainly do have a lot of examples around you to be scared of."

Bryce laughed and nodded and sat quietly for a second. "Do you miss him?"

"Every second of the day," I confided. "And I miss Henry."

"That should tell you everything you need to know," Bryce said, smiling.

"I think he's given up. I didn't respond to any of his texts or calls. Did you want to come to check out the place I signed the lease on?" I asked, trying to change the subject.

The truth was that I wasn't sure I was ready for the devastating heartbreak that could come with pursuing this relationship. I'd already gotten a taste of it after Henry asked that very important question, and we were both very ill-prepared.

"Sure. If that's your way of saying you're done talking about James, I'll take the hint."

I laughed, standing up. "Good. I appreciate that about you."

I needed this change, and I was pretty excited to show it off to someone. My sisters were all tired of seeing it, and Brad was the one who came with me last week to give me the thumbs-up. As we turned onto the tree-lined street, my heart raced with anticipation. The evening sun painted the sky a brilliant shade of coral and peach, setting the perfect backdrop to introduce my new place.

Bryce looked as excited as I felt, which was nice to see. He'd been there when my apartment building burned down, and also when I found the temporary place I'd been staying in. It was nice to have friends who were in your corner, rooting for you.

"There it is." I pointed toward the Cape Cod style home sitting on the corner lot. It was so much more than I ever expected to be able to do, but it was as if the stars aligned.

"Can you believe this, Amelia?" Bryce asked. "I mean, look at that front yard! It's like something out of a dream. See? Good things can come out of really bad things."

"Uh-oh," I teased. "You're starting to sound like me."

Bryce laughed as I pulled in front of the house. "I'm

able to move in next week after the deep cleaning, but the landlord already gave me the keys since I promised to give her ten percent off her next few purchases at the store."

Bryce crawled out of the car that I was still borrowing from my parents and stretched while taking in my new place.

"You're going to love living here. You'll even be able to walk to work."

"I know. I'm so excited." I nodded, but I felt empty.

No matter how hard I tried to pretend that this was the most thrilling moment of recent events, it wasn't true. All I could think about was my night with James and how everything just felt right.

We were making such great headway dealing with things, and we were both standing on the precipice, on the verge of finally creating our own destiny.

It felt so freeing to put my fear aside for the first time in a long time. I remember looking into James' eyes as we made love, and he felt like home. He felt like my comfort.

And nothing had felt right since.

There was just an emptiness.

"Okay. Take me on a tour." He smiled at me, tugging on my hand to get me out of my funk.

The front yard was immaculate. A manicured lawn stretched around the house, and flower beds dotted the landscape in vibrant pops of red, purple, and white. A cobblestone pathway led us from a tiny gate to the porch, where a cozy white swing hung. It was perfection.

Except that it had too many bedrooms. I need two at the most, but it had four. I shrugged at the thought and let out a sigh.

"Come on, let's go inside. We don't need to just drool over the yard," Bryce teased. "We've got a whole house to explore!"

I laughed and nodded as we headed toward the oversized front door painted in a bright, shiny red. As we stepped inside, the cool air greeted us, providing relief from the summer heat. The foyer was spacious, with an elegant crystal chandelier hanging from the ceiling and pale peach wallpaper wrapped around the room. A staircase had been tucked to the side, leading up to the second floor. I could just imagine wrapping Christmas garland around it this winter.

Usually, that thought would get me excited, but the thought just hung in my mind.

"It's a really great floorplan," I explained as we ventured into the living room.

The high ceilings and tall windows allowed natural light to flood the room. The walls were painted a soothing shade of pale blue, and the room opened into the kitchen, which was equally light and bright. The sparkling white counters and backsplash were a dream.

But all I could think about were James and Henry.

It would be so fun to make chocolate chip cookies with him on that island. I could imagine him sitting on top with a spatula, trying to sneak licks off a spoon.

"Imagine movie nights here," Bryce mused. "We can just wander over for popcorn refills."

I nodded, forcing a smile onto my lips.

"The backyard sold me on it," I told him, motioning for him to follow me.

I opened the sliding glass doors, which led us to a sprawling outdoor patio. A wooden deck extended from the house, and beyond it, a turquoise swimming pool glistened in the sunlight. It even came with a safety gate. The irony did not escape me.

Bryce let out a low whistle. "This is an amazing find, Amelia."

"It is. The landlord said they were thinking about selling next year but wanted to rent it for a year while they thought about it."

"Wow." Bryce nodded.

"You know what this means, right? Pool parties for the three weeks of summer we get here."

I chuckled and shook my head. "Our summers aren't that short. We just tell everyone they are so they don't move here."

Bryce grinned as we went back inside, and I showed him the upstairs and the four bedrooms. The primary bedroom had an amazing bath, with an even more amazing bathtub.

"The truth is that I know I probably won't be able to afford this place when they sell, and it will be a total pain to move again, but I just couldn't resist at least pretending for a year that it's mine. It's like a dream."

"Nothing wrong with that," Bryce said, glancing at his phone. "This place is great. I can't wait until you invite me back."

A funny look came over Bryce's face.

"What? Is it Herman?" I joked.

"No, but..." He licked his bottom lip and glanced outside. "I wish there were a place we could sit down and talk."

I laughed nervously. "Didn't we do enough of that over tea?"

He smiled and nodded. "It's about James."

Panic set in, and it felt like my heart stopped. "What do you mean? Is he okay?"

"Yeah. I'm sure he's fine. It's actually about his mom.

I know why she couldn't continue to raise him."

It was like the earth fell away beneath me, and I was floating into a terrible spiral.

"What are you talking about?" I asked as my mouth turned completely dry.

He drew a breath and motioned for me to follow him. Bryce went down a few stairs and sat down, motioning for me to do the same.

"I was just waiting to hear back from my mom before I told you."

"Told me what?" I stared at him in disbelief.

No one knew about James' mom. Why would Bryce, of all people, have answers?

"This is going to be hard to hear, but I think it might explain a lot, maybe give him some closure." He sucked in a breath and shook his head. "Or it might make it worse."

"Please just tell me," I said, searching Bryce's expression for any clues.

"You know my aunt I mentioned at the park?"

I nodded.

"She's actually in jail. Federal prison, to be exact."

My eyes widened. "I had no idea. I'm so sorry."

He frowned. "Don't be sorry. She should be there."

"I just…I just had no idea."

"Yeah, it's not something we exactly like to scream from the rooftops."

"How does that relate to James' mom? Was she in jail too?"

"Oh, no. Not at all." He let out a sigh. "But she ran with a really bad crowd for a very short amount of time. She hung out with my aunt a bit too much, and when she was young and in this rebellion phase, she slept with a guy."

"James' father?"

Bryce shook his head. "No, not yet. Her first boyfriend happened to be a man who is ruthless, unforgiving, and really bad, Amelia."

I cocked my head slightly as I tried to understand what Bryce was talking about. "What do you mean bad?"

"He was a murderer. He *is* a murderer, I should emphasize." Bryce shoved his hands over his head and locked eyes on me. "By all accounts, James' mom was a sweetheart, a good kid who just wanted to rebel a little."

I nodded.

"But she fell into a really bad crowd, and she got scared, rightfully so. She completely ended it with the guy and moved on."

"And your aunt?"

He rolled his eyes. "She's never learned and will be

an old lady when she sees the light of day."

"Okay," My voice trailed off, uncertain where this was going.

"Anyway, James' mom moved on and fell in love with James' dad. She'd been with him for several years and never heard from her first boyfriend and thought she'd left the past behind her."

A burning knot formed in the pit of my stomach.

"She had James and was so happy."

I nodded, almost wishing he wouldn't go on.

"And then one day, the old boyfriend showed up at her house. The reason she hadn't heard from him was because he'd been in prison for years. He went ballistic when he saw that she was with someone else. It didn't matter the number of restraining orders, security systems, or police calls, her ex wouldn't stop harassing her."

"Oh, no," I said softly, already knowing what he was going to say.

"Her ex killed James' dad and threatened anyone related to him would be next."

Tears pricked my eyes as I thought about James' mother.

"They caught him pretty quickly, but after only a few years in jail, he got out on a technicality."

My hands rose to my mouth. "When James was seven."

"Yeah." Bryce pressed his lips together. "She did everything she could to protect him and hide that she'd even had him. When the police couldn't help her, she knew what she had to do."

I used my sleeve to dab the tears away. I couldn't even think straight.

The love she felt for James all these years.

The loss James felt for equal years.

Just none of it made sense.

"How did your aunt know all of this?" I asked.

"There's like this crazy criminal communication thing that happens in jails and prisons. I don't even know other than to say that my aunt would still run with that same crowd if she were on the outside."

As the story settled all around me like little bombs going off, I didn't know what to do or think.

I wanted to scream to James that his mom's love wasn't a lie. It was real, far more real than we could ever imagine.

Of course, it would never make up for what he'd missed, but the pain was surely equal on both sides.

I looked up at Bryce. "How long have you known

this?"

He shook his head. "Just a few days. It took a lot of pleading for my mom to reach out to my aunt. They're not exactly on friendly terms."

"Wow." I nodded slowly. "Thanks for digging around so much for me. I don't even know what to say or do."

Bryce nodded and pulled my hands into his. "I'd start by calling him."

CHAPTER TWENTY-SIX

James

"Mom, you will not believe what I just found out about James' mother," Amelia said, nearly panting from sprinting into the store.

She barged in through the front door and could barely catch her breath. I glanced around to see Dottie sprawled under a table and waited for her to find her mom and me.

"Seriously, Mom. I need to talk to you," she said again. "This will blow your mind."

She made her way through the antique-lined shelves when her mom turned around slowly.

The expression on Amelia's face said everything.

She didn't expect me to be here.

To hear.

I gulped down the anger that nipped at my tongue and steadied my breathing.

What could she possibly know about my mom?

"What have you heard about my mother, Amelia?" My voice sounded sterner than I intended, but the emotions raging through me were raw.

First, I came here to apologize and try to earn Amelia's trust back, and then I heard her running in like the town crier about my family.

It didn't seem like the Amelia I knew at all.

"I just…" She stopped herself. "I'm sorry. It probably sounded horrible."

I took a step forward. "It didn't sound good."

"I—" She looked away and dabbed away some tears as her mother went to her.

"It's okay. Take a deep breath. It will all be okay."

Amelia sniffled and shook her head. "It won't be okay. James, it's not okay."

The confusion rolling through me only made me angrier.

What did she think she knew?

What was she talking about?

Her mom slid her hand along Amelia's dark hair. "Honey, I should go. I'll let you two talk."

Amelia shook her head, bringing her gaze to mine. "No, Mom. I'd like you to stay."

Her mom glanced at me and grimaced as I brought my eyes back to Amelia. She looked so frail suddenly, and timid. This wasn't the Amelia I knew.

"Amelia, please tell me what you've heard." I drew a breath and debated about saying the words I didn't want to say. "Please, just tell me, and you don't have to see me ever again."

Her green eyes whipped to mine, and she looked like she was going to get violently ill. Her mom held her hand as Amelia shook her head.

"Your mom did what she did because she loved you. I swear," she choked out.

"I'll be the judge of that."

"It's true," she said between sobs.

As the first word came out of her mouth, her own mother gasped and held her tight as Amelia relayed the story about my parents.

About my mom.

About her love for me.

It felt like my world was spinning.

The hatred I felt immediately refreshed with confusion and guilt.

And regret.

So much regret.

"She hid you to protect you, James." Amelia ran her sleeve over her face. "She loved you more than herself."

The words were like a direct stab to the heart. All these years, I'd spent my life weaving an intricate web of falsehoods to protect myself. I shielded myself from love so that I didn't have to have it ripped away again. I pretended I'd never been loved so I didn't have to deal with the pain of losing it.

Amelia's eyes steadied on mine, but I couldn't move.

I was in shock. The world that had been constructed around me had destroyed me rather than built me up. I felt a rage like never before.

"And that man is dead?" I asked, knowing it was my one saving grace for Henry.

"He is," Amelia said softly. "He died right before your mother passed away."

I ran my fingers over the many days of growth from not shaving and stared at the shelves of antiques.

"When I held those letters, I knew she loved you. I could feel the adoration rolling off the pages," Amelia said quietly. But the moment those words left her mouth, I could see the regret. She started to apologize, but she stopped and turned around.

Before I had a chance to stop her, she ran out the front door, and I realized my life would never be the same.

"I'm sorry, James. No child should ever have to endure what you have." Her mom let out a soft sigh. "And no mother should ever be forced to choose between their child's safety and their own love and sacrifice."

My existence no longer felt real. I just felt like I was in a fog. I could have seen my mom. I could have connected on some level. I was nearing forty. Why couldn't I be given the chance to defend myself?

"She didn't have to protect me from that man. I'm nearly forty. I could have taken care of things," I said gruffly to no one in particular.

"And Henry?" Amelia's mom asked quietly.

My eyes connected with hers, and I felt an emptiness that I hadn't felt since before Henry.

I let out a deep sigh and shook my head. "No, you're right. I—"

"This man had already killed your father. His threats weren't vague and meaningless. She'd spent a lifetime ensuring your safety. She wouldn't be foolish enough to slip up at the end."

I didn't say anything for a few seconds as all the

thoughts rolled around in my head. It was like a bomb went off, and then the person who detonated it ran away.

She ran away.

"I know Amelia means well, and she thinks she can feel things in those letters or other items, but—"

Amelia's mom straightened up and swept her hand forward to stop me from continuing. "She doesn't think it, James. She knows it. She's very perceptive. Why do you think she's in a ball of tears somewhere right now? Because she feels your pain like few others can. Her ex saw it as a weakness. I'd like to believe you see it as her greatest strength."

"It just seems…strange," I said, exhausted.

"Life is full of strangeness." Amelia's mom's eyes connected with mine. "It's full of odd coincidences and even stranger facts. Sometimes, the found objects we sell were never lost at all and are only strange to the people they weren't meant for."

I let out a silent breath and nodded.

"Things aren't lost until someone realizes they're missing. They're not found until they're looked for." She reached over and patted my shoulder. "And sometimes, you don't even know they're missing until you've found them. Kind of like love."

"I never thought of myself as a spiritual man, but then I had Henry. I realized that there would forever be questions that I didn't have answers for and that all I could do was show him the love I have for him. I just don't know if it's enough. I hope it will be, but I know how much I missed my mother's love."

Her mom looked at me tenderly. "I would do anything for my children. Anything. The love I have for each of them is so profound that it's unexplainable to someone who doesn't understand that kind of connection, and some of my actions to protect them might be considered inexcusable, but that's only if someone didn't know the reasons behind them."

I stared at the vase I didn't take home and suddenly felt even more drawn to it as if it held the history I never knew I'd been looking for.

Amelia was right.

"It sounds like your mom made a sacrifice that few would ever understand. She needed to protect you above anything and everything else, including her own happiness." She reached over and squeezed my hand. "Your safety became her priority no matter the cost and no matter the heartache, and the fact that she knew that the price of you thinking she didn't love you was still more absolute in keeping you alive shows that she loved you more than herself. It was never a case of her not loving you. She didn't abandon you. She saved you, James."

CHAPTER TWENTY-SEVEN

Amelia

"I didn't think it was possible, but this flower arrangement is even bigger than the last one," Emily said, laughing.

I'd just moved into my new house and happened to have a floral arrangement the size of my new Hyundai on my front porch.

I glanced behind my shoulder to see Emily snickering before I bent down to read the card.

Amelia,

I'm so sorry, and I'll spend my lifetime trying to make it up to you if that's what it takes. I never should have shut you out when Henry asked that question. It was innocent, and I was anything but. I hope that I can earn your trust back because my life has been absolutely miserable without you, apart from my adorable, wonderful son. He makes it great, but you know what I mean.

> *I miss you. I love you. I want to make things better.*
> *With all my love and more,*
> *James and Henry (See what I did there? Did it work?)*

I chuckled as I slid the card back in place, and without realizing it, Emily brushed a tear off my cheek.

"When are you going to believe him?" she asked as I pushed open my front door to reveal the floral arrangement from yesterday in my foyer.

"When I get one more for my bedroom. This new one is going to go in my kitchen." I winked at Emily, and she laughed.

"That's playing dirty."

"Well, if that isn't something," the low growl of James' voice nearly unhinged me.

I spun around to see him standing on the cobblestone pathway leading to my door.

"You can't blame a girl for trying." I smiled, feeling a smattering of butterflies collide in my belly just from the sight of him.

"I think the garlic fries are calling my name over at Milo's," Emily muttered as she gave me a quick hug and found herself walking down the sidewalk. "I'll see ya tomorrow."

I smiled at my sister and drew a deep breath, trying to regain my footing. There was always something about James that made me feel a little off-kilter, but in the best way possible.

Like now, his lips tugged into a delicious smile as his eyes ran up and down my body.

"It's been too long," he said quietly, walking toward me on the porch.

"I'm sorry about how you found out about your mom and your dad."

His eyes stayed on mine, and he nodded. "I wouldn't have wanted to find out any other way. It was you who needed to deliver that message to me. I see that now."

Surprise dashed through me. "You do?"

"I'm beginning to realize a lot of things."

"Tell me," I said as he stood only a foot away.

"I did a little experiment with your mom."

My brows furrowed. "Okay. Not where I thought we were going with this."

He chuckled.

"She told me you'd finished emptying the last of the storage containers from my mom's house."

I nodded, wishing that the process would have gone much slower.

"And I went through the store with her and picked out all of the items that I felt called to me on some level."

My eyes widened. "You're being serious?"

"I am." He drew a breath. "Needless to say, there wasn't one item that didn't come from my mom's house. And I swear to you, it was like a magnet pulling me home, pulling me to those pieces. It was like you've said, a heart of curiosities just filing away over a lifetime. It was like what my mind refused to see or believe, my heart knew on some level."

"Your heart knew she always loved you," I said softly.

"Yeah. It did." James' gaze fell to my lips, and he brought it back up. "And I'm so sorry. I'm so sorry for ever making you feel unworthy or like you couldn't be Henry's mom or that I had any doubts about you or us. You are my home. My heart is content when we're together."

My eyes widened as I thought about my dad's words to me not so long ago. I took a step forward and placed my hands on James' chest.

"Being with you is like coming home, James Edwards. You're my home."

He swept his mouth down to mine and kissed me gently. I could taste a hint of peppermint as I thought about how deeply I'd missed being in his arms.

I took a step back and nearly fell over the flower arrangement before James caught me in his arms. "I got you. I always will. I'll never let you go."

His words danced in my heart and made a home there as I looked into his eyes.

"Can we start over? Maybe rewind back to the night I didn't get my bratwurst and potato salad?"

James held me tight and laughed, nodding. "Absolutely. Anything you want."

"And can I still get another flower arrangement? It would be so cool to have one in my bedroom too."

James nuzzled his nose on mine. "Anything for you."

"Do you mind bringing that one into the kitchen, and I can show you around?"

He kissed me once more and then bent down to carry the gigantic arrangement inside.

"The kitchen is right this way." I smiled over my shoulder at him, and he grinned, waggling his brows.

"No rush. Just taking in the view."

My cheeks flushed under his gaze. "Oh, really? And what's the view like?"

"Incredible. Luscious. Intoxicating. Addicting." He laughed. "Should I go on?"

I glanced behind me as we made our way into the kitchen. "Right there will be perfect."

His lips curled into a charming smirk, and he leaned forward after setting down the arrangement. His eyes held mine with an intensity that sent shivers down my spine.

"The view," he began, his voice a velvety whisper, "is absolutely breathtaking. The way the light plays on your hair, the curve of your lips when you smile."

"Are you trying to seduce me?" I teased. "Because I think I'm owed a dinner first."

"Brats and potato salad?"

I chuckled as my heart fluttered.

His words ignited a spark of desire that danced in my belly, but it was the way he was looking at me that made my world tilt off its axis.

No man had ever made me feel the way James made me feel.

It was more than feeling like I was home with him. It was that I knew we could face any challenge ahead. I knew we were more united together than apart.

I nodded with a smirk. "Yeah. Brats and potato salad."

He chuckled as his fingers traced an invisible pattern on my chest. "I love you, Amelia. I hope you know that."

"I love you more."

"I doubt that. I love hard."

"I love harder," I teased.

He leaned closer, his voice low and enticing. "If it's a game, I will win. You make my world brighter. You make my son's world sweeter. We need you in our lives."

The atmosphere shifted into a cocoon of intimacy. It was as if we were the only two people in the world. Our connection was so palpable, I swore I could see electricity zapping through the air.

"Flattery will get you everywhere."

James' smoldering gaze melted me in place as his fingers brushed against mine, sending another jolt of electricity through my veins. "Oh, I have no doubt about that."

Everything about James was intoxicating—his confidence, his tenderness, his heart.

As I brought in a deep breath, I knew the air was charged with an unspoken invitation.

I leaned in a little closer and grazed his ear "So, are you trying to sleep with me?"

I stood back, watching his expression turn into nothing but mischief.

His gaze dipped briefly to my lips before returning to meet my eyes. "I'm just trying to invite you to dinner."

The tension between us was excruciatingly delightful.

With a coy smile, I leaned against the island as my fingers played with some white roses.

He reached across the table to trace the back of his fingers against my hand, and a stimulating wave of anticipation coursed through me.

"Amelia, I need to know."

My brows rose. "Yeah?"

"Will you forgive me?"

"There's nothing to forgive." I shook my head as he stepped closer. "We've been doing the best we can in a completely new arena."

He cocked his head slightly. "I never should have backed off from you that night. I just heard that question from Henry and panicked, and I shouldn't have."

I shook my head and smiled. "It's okay. It's all okay."

"Why do you say that?"

"Because if we hadn't gone through that, I don't think we ever would have found out about your mom. The only reason Bryce had his mom reach out to the estranged aunt was because he could see how much turmoil I was in. If none of that happened, you'd still think she didn't love you."

"You never cease to amaze me, Amelia." He cupped his fingers around my chin and tilted my face so gently before bringing his mouth to mine.

Every brush of his lips and sweep of his tongue shot a jolt of desire through me, and I knew I didn't care if I ever got the brats and potato salad. I just needed James Edwards back in my life.

We fit.

We all fit perfectly well.

CHAPTER TWENTY-EIGHT

James

"What about my happiness?" Henry asked, stomping his foot.

"Where in the world did you learn a sentence like that?" I frowned, glancing at Lucas and Emily, who suddenly stared at the apple trees. "Is this what happens when you two babysit him?"

Amelia wandered over with a caramel apple and leaned down. "Here ya go, fella."

I let out an exasperated sigh. "He wants cotton candy now. He says I'm not taking into account his happiness."

Amelia's brows rose. "He said that?"

"Not in so many words. Where did he pick up that kind of question?"

Emily rolled her eyes. "Okay, so it might have slipped out when Lucas dropped him off at my house to babysit so he could go out on a date."

Lucas' gaze bored into Emily. "I'm only going out on the date because you've turned me down seventeen hundred times."

"You two sound like an angry, old married couple."

Henry giggled and pointed at them. "Old married couple. You're old married couple."

I squeezed Henry's shoulders lightly and tried to distract him away from the cotton candy machine.

"The first weekend is a huge success," I said happily, glancing around the bustling orchard.

A breeze swept through right when Amelia went to take a sip of her cider, and her scarf flew in her face. I quickly pushed it down so she wouldn't spill the cider everywhere.

The afternoon autumn sun cast a warm, golden glow over the enchanting apple orchard, setting the stage for a day of amazing festivities. As I turned to check on Henry, the sweet scent of ripe apples filled the air, mixing with the anticipation that hummed all around. The festival was in full swing, and it promised a day filled with joy, laughter, and a touch of magic.

My cousins and I did a great job putting this together.

My parents would be proud.

I bent down to Henry and pointed at the petting zoo. "Ready to go over there and see some animals?"

Henry nodded as he wrestled the caramel apple into his mouth, and we all walked over to the bustling petting zoo. The handlers greeted us at the entrance as Henry took in everything from fluffy rabbits to gentle lambs. All of the children's faces lit up with wonder as they stroked soft fur and giggled at the playful antics of rogue chickens or mooing cows. I couldn't help but smile as a pair of mischievous goats bumped heads, vying for attention from an eager group of kids. Henry giggled and clapped his hands, which dislodged the caramel apple out of his hands and into the dirt.

Before Henry even had a chance to cry, Amelia swooped in and grabbed the sticky mess out of the mud and handed it off to Emily, who made a relay to the cotton candy stand and appeared before the first tear had shed.

As Henry wandered over to pet a tiny lamb, I wrapped my arm around Amelia and pulled her close. "You've made this day even more amazing."

"Aww, you and your cousins did all the hard work." She grinned, watching two chickens dance around a group of kids. "I just hid Henry at the house this morning."

"I've never seen his eyes so huge."

She nodded and pressed her head against my shoulder. "It was the cutest thing I've ever seen."

"I'm just glad I get to share it with you," I said softly.

"There isn't anyone else in the world I belong with and there's nowhere else I'd rather be." She straightened and turned to face me. "And I feel like I've been dropping hints left and right about it, and I get it if the answer is no…"

I tired to hide my smile and play like I didn't know what she was talking about.

"Yeah?" I asked.

"But the house I'm renting has four bedrooms, and you're always saying how the orchard place is too huge and reminds you of living at your grandparents' house…"

I chuckled. "Well, because it is my grandparents' house."

She grinned and held my hand. "Right, so I'm just going to come out and say it."

"Would you and Henry make my house your house when you're on this island?"

I squeezed her hand and smiled. "Are you sure you'd actually want two men living with you? We're messy. No, we're dirty." I pointed over at Henry who now had cotton candy smashed onto his cheeks along with several pieces of bark and something else I'd rather not think about.

She glanced at Henry and chuckled. "I'm sure."

"Every once in a while, he might still miss," I explained. "You know… he's potty trained, but…"

Amelia's grin only widened. "I can deal."

"Then there's only one other thing we have to do," I said softly.

Her brows rose, and she nodded. "You mean get Henry to agree to it?"

"You got it."

Amelia let out a low whistle. "This could be tough. Let's wait until I get him sugar drunk."

I laughed as Henry wandered over, scowling.

"What happened?"

"Pig burp."

Amelia chuckled and held out her hand and received a very slimy, dirty little boy's hand in exchange. "Let's go explore. Your dad did an amazing job putting this together."

I couldn't help but love Amelia even more for how she was with my son. If I could have handpicked a woman, it would have been her. It was almost like there was some other force determined to get us together, some other destiny that wouldn't be crossed, dropping hints until we couldn't ignore them any longer. Okay, Amelia and her family had definitely worn off on me.

As we wandered down the path, the comforting aroma of freshly baked apple pies wafted through the air. The apple pie contest was in full swing as a line of happy bakers displayed their creations and handed out slices to the judges.

Children's laughter mingled with the neighing of ponies filled the air. The line for pony rides grew by the second.

I bent down to Henry. "Did you want to ride a pony?"

"I'm scared."

Amelia kneeled down and touched his chin. "You don't have to be scared. I know it's a new adventure, but I'll be right there with you. I'll hold onto you the moment you're in the saddle. We'll be a team."

Henry's eyes brightened as his smile grew. "Thank you, Mommy Meelya."

Amelia's eyes darted to mine, but I didn't run. She didn't freeze. We just embraced this next step of our relationship, and if that meant he had a Mommy Meelya right now, then so be it.

Amelia picked up Henry, and we walked to the ponies adorned with bright orange and white ribbons and yellow flowers. They trotted along with their eager riders holding on tight. It was a scene straight out of a storybook, and I finally started to let myself believe in fairy tales.

I glanced over to see the orchard from this vantage point. We were higher on the hill, and row upon rows of apple-laden trees stretched out as far as the eye could see. We had over ten varieties ready to be picked, and it brought back such amazing memories.

Memories that I'd fought so hard to keep at bay until recently. Now, I treasured each new one that resurfaced. And soon, I might even be ready to read my mom's diary, but I didn't want to rush it. I was still processing everything I'd learned a couple of months ago. But I had read my diary from when I was little, and it brought back so many memories, and Henry had even played with some of my toys Amelia had found in the storage container.

Amelia squeezed my arm as I watched families armed with baskets and plenty of smiles roaming into the orchard. There was nothing like picking your own plump, juicy apples.

Nearby, the first-annual Island Pet Contest was in full swing, with pets of all shapes and sizes strutting their stuff on a makeshift stage. A proud Dachshund sported a Hawaiian lei, while a parrot perched regally on its owner's shoulder. There was even a tortoise ambling along with a tiny grass skirt tied around its shell. I have to admit that one looked humiliated. But there were two frontrunners, Bryce's toothless Doberman and Dottie, the Antiquarian.

"The judge has a tough task ahead," Amelia whispered, glancing at the pet contest.

"Yeah. I wouldn't want to be the judge."

Amelia nodded and ruffled Henry's hair and smiled at him with such an endearing look. She was so motherly, even to me.

Right when Henry was about to be placed on his pony, a man's voice echoed through the air.

The winner of the pet contest was about to be announced.

Amelia looked at me and then over to the stage where her mom stood proudly with Dottie. Herman kept trying to sniff the pug, and every once in a while, it looked like Dottie was into it.

But suddenly, out of nowhere, the crowd gasped.

All heads turned to Amelia's brother, who was walking in with Oscar as if he owned the place. The turtle owner picked up his reptile and held him close while Amelia's mom scowled at Oscar and lifted Dottie into her arms.

Brad was completely oblivious to the fear that cat struck in any and all living beings.

"You okay?" Amelia whispered when she caught me rubbing my cheek.

"Yeah. Sorry. Flashbacks."

Amelia chuckled as Brad placed his cat on a leash in the center of the stage. The judge, who also happened to be the town vet and mayor, glared at Oscar. They'd obviously met before.

Emily and Lucas wandered over to the stage as the judge tried to explain that Brad was too late to enter, but Brad held up a contestant number.

The judge nodded and circled around Oscar while Herman started getting a little jumpy. A hiss ran through the crowd in shock as Herman got away from Bryce and charged toward Oscar.

Oscar didn't move.

"Oh, no. I can't watch," Amelia said, closing her eyes.

The crowd hushed as Herman opened his mouth and grabbed the nape of the cat's neck with his toothless jaw and carried him over to the water-dunk tank.

"What's going on?" Amelia asked.

"You gotta see this."

She opened her eyes right when the Doberman stood on his hind legs and raised the cat over the plexiglass cage and dunked Oscar right into the water.

The screech could be heard for miles around as Oscar's ears laid flat and his eyes scowled at the crowd. Dottie made her way over and sat in front of the dunk tank, as did all the other town pets.

"Herman knew Oscar was a bully," Amelia said in awe.

"I'm speechless."

"You can't tell me there aren't other things in our universe at play."

I laughed and shook my head. "I really am speechless."

The judge cleared his throat. "Okay, we have a tie. Ladies and gentlemen, we now have an honorary king and queen of Marigold Island. The winners are Dottie and Herman."

Her mom shrieked with joy as Brad fished out a very defeated Oscar from the tank. A gal rushed over with a towel, but to my surprise, Oscar didn't fight.

"Okay, no words." I shook my head.

"I still don't trust that cat," Amelia said, waving at her mom, who brought Dottie over in her arms.

"I feel bad for Brad. He just doesn't know what a terror Oscar is." My mom shook her head and rolled her eyes. "But, we all know who the queen is, don't we?"

Amelia chuckled as her mom's brows rose in surprise.

"I'll be darned." Her mom grinned at me and then back at Amelia.

Henry was tugging on Amelia's scarf.

"I thought you lost that broach I'd given you." She smiled at Amelia and nodded slowly. "Interesting. Wouldn't you say?"

Amelia shrugged. I glanced down to see a beautiful jade apple pinned to Amelia's scarf.

"Did Amelia tell you the story of that pin?"

I shook my head while Amelia coyly smiled.

"Well, when each of my children were born, I gave them a piece of jewelry that would guide their choices."

Amelia blushed.

"Choices for what?"

"Well, finding a partner." Her mom shook her head and laughed. "It's funny. Now, it's clear as day, but I never saw it coming."

"Saw what?" I asked, glancing at the apple on her scarf.

"The broach was the vintage piece I chose for Amelia. An apple. Curious, isn't it?" Her mom didn't say another word but wandered off to find her husband as Amelia's gaze met mine.

"There are no coincidences in your family, are there?"

She laughed, and her shoulders brushed her ears. "There don't seem to be, but I never saw it coming."

I chuckled and shook my head. "Just like I didn't see that apple you lobbed at me all those years ago."

"Hardee-har-har." She rolled her eyes and sucked on her bottom lip. "I'm just full of surprises."

My gaze fell to Amelia's lips, and I couldn't help but pull her into my arms and kiss her because I knew I just fell even harder for the woman who understood the heart of curiosities more than I ever could, and something told me that Henry and I would never be alone again.

Dear Readers,

I hope you loved Amelia and James as much as I did. There's just something about this island that I can't wait to continue to explore. I'm so excited about this new series, and I can't thank you enough for reading the first in the Curiosity Bay Series. It was so much fun to write.

I'm looking forward to sharing Emily's story next in *Wilds of the Heart*! It's available for pre-order. Until then, you can read the Sunshine Breakfast Club or any of the other series that I have available to binge on most retailers and some are also available on my own website at www.kariceboltonbooks.com.

Feel free to join me over at my Facebook group at Karice Bolton Book Buzz or like my page for updates, contests, and sneak peeks!

Warmest wishes,
Karice

BOOKS BY KARICE BOLTON

CURIOSITY BAY SERIES

HEART OF CURIOSITIES

WILDS OF THE HEART (Coming 1-1-24)

SUNSHINE BREAKFAST CLUB

DASH OF LOVE

SPRINKLE OF LOVE
PINCH OF LOVE
CHRISTMAS OF LOVE

MR. MISTAKE SERIES

MR. MISTAKE
MR. ACCIDENT
MR. WRONG
MR. RIGHT

ISLAND COUNTY SERIES

FINDING LOVE IN FORGOTTEN COVE
LOVE REDONE IN HIDDEN HARBOR
TANGLED LOVE ON PELICAN POINT
FOREVER LOVE ON FIREWEED ISLAND
TEMPTING LOVE ON HOLLY LANE
CHANCE AT LOVE ON MYSTIC BAY
IRRESISTIBLE LOVE AT SILVER FALLS
LUCKY IN LOVE ON HOUND ISLAND
MISTLETOE MISCHIEF

ACCIDENTAL LOVE ON MEADOW COVE LANE
DISCOVERING LOVE ON CRANBERRY LANE
CHRISTMAS ON FIREWEED
IMAGINING LOVE ON WILLOW ROAD
CHRISTMAS CRUSH ON FIREWEED

BEYOND LOVE SERIES
BEYOND CONTROL
BEYOND DOUBT
BEYOND REASON
BEYOND INTENT
BEYOND CHANCE
BEYOND PROMISE
BEYOND the MISTLETOE

CLOUDBERRY INN SERIES
IMAGINING YOU
REMEMBERING YOU
LEAVING YOU
LOVING YOU

SILVER RIDGE SERIES
A HAPPY TRUTH ABOUT LOVE
A LITTLE SECRET ABOUT LOVE
A FUNNY THING ABOUT LOVE
A SURPRISING FACT ABOUT LOVE
A SIMPLE WISH ABOUT LOVE

LUKE FLETCHER SERIES
HIDDEN SINS
BURIED SINS
REDEMPTION

MIA

BLOOD TORN DUET
BLOOD TORN
BLOOD CURSED

V MAFIA SERIES
BLAKE
DEVIN
JAXSON

THE WITCH AVENUE SERIES
LONELY SOULS
ALTERED SOULS
RELEASED SOULS
SHATTERED SOULS

THE WATCHERS TRILOGY
AWAKENING
LEGIONS
CATACLYSM
TAKEN NOVELLA (A Watchers Prequel)

AFTERWORLD SERIES
RecruitZ
AlibiZ
UprisingZ